AWAKENED BY HER DESERT CAPTOR

BY

ABBY GREEN

MILLS &
BOON

First published in Great Britain 2016
By Mills & Boon, an imprint of HarperCollins *Publishers*
1 London Bridge Street, London, SE1 9GF

Large Print edition 2016

© 2016 Abby Green

ISBN: 978-0-263-26207-0

Our policy is to use papers that are natural, renewable
and recyclable products and made from wood grown
in sustainable forests. The logging and manufacturing
processes conform to the legal environmental regulations
of the country of origin.

Printed and bound in Great Britain
by CPI Antony Rowe, Chippenham, Wiltshire

This is for Iona, Heidi, Fiona and Susan…
my support network. Love you ladies.

PROLOGUE

THE PRIEST'S EYES widened as he took in the spectacle approaching down the aisle, but to give him his due he didn't falter in his words, which came as automatically to him as breathing.

It was a slim figure, dressed from head to toe in black leather, the face obscured by a motorcycle helmet's visor. The person stopped a few feet behind the couple standing before the priest, and his eyes widened even further as a young woman emerged from under the motorcycle helmet as she took it off and placed it under one arm.

Long red hair cascaded dramatically over her shoulders just as he heard himself say the words, '...or for ever hold your peace...' a little more faintly than usual.

The woman's face was pale, but determined. And also very, very beautiful. Even a priest could appreciate that.

Silence descended, and then her voice rang out loud and clear in the huge church. 'I object to this wedding. Because last night this man shared my bed.'

CHAPTER ONE

Six months previously...

SYLVIE DEVEREUX STEELED herself for what was undoubtedly to be another bruising encounter with her father and stepmother. She reminded herself as she walked up the stately drive that she was only making an appearance for her half-sister's sake. The one person in the world she would do anything for.

Lights spilled from the enormous Richmond house, and soft classic jazz came from the live band in the back garden, where a marquee was just visible. Grant Lewis's midsummer party was an annual fixture on the London social scene, presided over each year by his smiling piranha of a wife, Catherine Lewis—Sylvie's stepmother and mother to her younger half-sister, Sophie.

A shape appeared at the front door and an excited squeal presaged a blur of blonde as Sophie Lewis launched herself at her older sister. Sylvie dropped her bag and clung on, struggling to remain upright, huffing a chuckle into her sister's soft, silky hair.

'I guess that means you're pleased to see me, Soph?'

Sophie, younger by six years, pulled back with a grimace on her pretty face. 'You have *no* idea. Mother is even worse than usual—literally throwing me into the arms of every eligible man—and Father is holed up in his study with some sheikh dude who is probably the grimmest guy I've ever seen, but also the most gorgeous—pity it's wasted on—'

'*There* you are, Sophie—'

The voice broke off as Sylvie's stepmother realised who her sister's companion was. They were almost at the front door now, and the lights backlit Catherine Lewis's slender Chanel-clad figure and blonde hair, coiffed to within an inch of its life.

Her mouth tightened with distaste. 'Oh, it's you. We didn't think you'd make it.'

You mean you'd hoped I wouldn't make it, Sylvie desisted from saying. She forced a bright smile and pushed down the hurt that had no place here any more. She should be over this by now, at the grand age of twenty-eight. 'Delighted as ever to see you, Catherine.'

Her sister squeezed her arm in silent support. Catherine stepped back minutely, clearly reluctant to admit Sylvie into her own family home. 'Your father is having a meeting with a guest. He should be free shortly.'

Then her stepmother frowned under the bright lights, taking in what Sylvie was wearing. Sylvie felt a fleeting sense of satisfaction at the expected wave of disapproval. But then she also felt incredibly weary...tired of this constant battle she fought.

'You're welcome to change in Sophie's room if you wish. Clearly you've come straight from one of your...er...shows in Paris.'

She had actually. A matinée show. But she'd left work dressed in jeans and a perfectly respectable T-shirt. She'd changed on the train on the way. And suddenly her weariness fled.

She stuck a hand on her hip and cocked it out. 'It was a gift from a fan,' she purred. 'I know how much you like your guests to dress up.'

The dress really belonged to her flatmate, the far more glamorous Giselle, who was a couple of bra sizes smaller than her. Sylvie had borrowed it, knowing full well the effect it would have. She knew it was childish to feel this urge to shock constantly, but right now it was worth it.

Just then there was movement nearby, and Sylvie followed her stepmother's look to see her father standing outside his office, which was just off the main entrance hall. She barely registered him, though. He was with a man—a tall, very broad, very dark man. The most arresting-looking man she'd ever seen. His face was all sculpted lean lines, not a hint of softness anywhere. Dark slashing brows. Grim indeed, if this was who Sophie had been talking about.

Power and charisma was a tangible force around him. And a very sexual magnetism. He was dressed in a light grey three-piece suit. Dark tie. Pristine. The white of his shirt made the darkness of his skin stand out even more. His hair was inky black, and short. His eyes were equally dark, and totally unreadable. She shivered slightly.

The two men were looking at her, and Sylvie didn't even have to see her father's face to know what his expression would be: a mix of old grief, disappointment and wariness.

'Ah, Sylvie, glad you could make it.'

She finally managed to drag her mesmerised gaze from the stranger to look at her father. She forced a bright smile and moved forward. 'Father—good to see you.'

His welcome was only slightly warmer than her stepmother's. A dry kiss on her cheek, avoiding her eyes. Old wounds smarted again, but Sylvie pushed them all down to erect the *don't care* façade she'd honed over years.

She looked up at the man and fluttered her eyelashes, flirting shamelessly. 'And who do we have *here*?'

With evident reluctance, Grant Lewis said, 'I'd like you to meet Arkim Al-Sahid. We're discussing a mutual business venture.'

The name rang a dim bell, but Sylvie couldn't focus on how she knew it. She put out her hand. 'Pleasure, I'm sure. But don't you find discussing business at a party so *dull*?'

She could almost feel the snap of her stepmother's censure from behind her, and heard something that sounded like a strangled snort from her sister. The man's expression had a faint sneer of disapproval now, and suddenly something deep inside Sylvie erupted to life.

It goaded her into moving even closer to the man, when every instinct urged her to turn and run fast. Her hand was still held out and his nostrils flared as he finally deigned to acknowledge her. His much bigger hand swallowed hers, and she was surprised to feel that his skin was slightly calloused as long fingers wrapped around hers.

Everything suddenly became muffled. As if a membrane had been dropped around the two of them. A pulse throbbed violently between her legs and a series of out-of-control reactions gripped her so fast she couldn't make sense of them. Heat, and a weakness in her lower belly and limbs. A melting sensation. An urge to move even closer and wind her arms around his neck, press herself against him, along with that urge to run, which was even stronger now.

Then he broke the connection with an abrupt move, extricating his hand from hers. Sylvie almost stumbled backwards, confused by what had happened. Not liking it at all.

'Pleasure, indeed.'

The man's voice was deep, with a slight American accent, and his tone said that it was anything but a pleasure. The sensual lines of his mouth were flat. That dark gaze glanced over her, dismissing her.

Immediately Sylvie felt cheaper than she'd ever felt in her life. She was very aware of how short her gold dress was—skimming the tops of her thighs. Her light jacket didn't provide much coverage. She was too voluptuous for the dress, and she felt every exposed inch of it now. She was also aware of the fall of her unruly hair, its natural red hue effortlessly loud and attention-seeking.

She made a living from wearing not much at all. And she'd grown a thick skin to hide her innate shyness. Yet right now this man's dismissal had blasted away that carefully built-up wall. Within mere seconds of meeting him—a total stranger.

Aghast to note that she was feeling a sense of rejection, when she'd developed an inbuilt defence mechanism against ever experiencing it again, Sylvie backed away.

Relief surged through her when her sister appeared, slid an arm through their father's and said with forced brightness, 'Come on, Daddy, your guests will be wondering where you are.'

She watched as her father, stepmother and sister walked off—along with the disturbing stranger who sent her barely a glance of acknowledgement.

On legs that felt absurdly shaky Sylvie finally followed the group outside and determined to stay out of that man's dangerous orbit, sticking close to Sophie and her group of friends.

A few hours later, though, she found herself craving a moment's peace—away from people getting progressively drunker, and away from the censorious gaze of her stepmother and the tension emanating from her father.

She found a quiet spot near the gazebo, where a river ran at the end of the garden. After sitting down on the grass and taking off her shoes she put her feet in the cool rushing water and breathed out a sigh.

It was only after she'd tipped her head back and had been contemplating the full moon, low in the sky, for a few seconds that she felt a nerve-tingling awareness that she wasn't alone.

She looked around just as a tall, dark shape moved in the shadows of a nearby tree. Stifling a scream, Sylvie sat up straight, heart pounding, and asked, 'Who's there?'

The shadow detached itself, revealing the other reason for her need to escape: so she could find an opportunity to dwell on why she'd had such a confusing and forcible reaction to the enigmatic stranger.

'You know exactly who's here,' came the arrogant response.

Sylvie could make out the glitter of those dark

eyes. Feeling seriously at a disadvantage, sitting down, she stood again and shoved her feet back into her shoes, her heels sinking into the soft earth, making her wobble.

'How much have you had to drink?' He sounded disgusted.

Anger at the unjust question had Sylvie putting her hands on her hips. 'A magnum of champagne—is that what you expect to hear?'

She'd actually had nothing to drink, because she was still on antibiotics to clear up a nagging out-of-season chest infection. Not that she was about to furnish *him* with that little domestic detail.

'For your information,' she said, 'I came here because I believed I'd be alone. So I'll leave you to your arrogant assumptions and get out of your way.'

Sylvie started to stalk off, only noticing then how close they were—close enough for Arkim Al-Sahid to reach out and touch her. Which was exactly what he did when her heel got caught in the soft earth again and she pitched forward into thin air with a cry of surprise.

He caught her arm in such a firm grip that she went totally off balance and was swung around directly into his chest, landing against him with a soft *oof.* Her first impression was of how hard he was—like a concrete block.

And how tall.

Sylvie forgot why she'd been leaving. 'Tell me,' she asked, more breathily than she would have liked, 'do you hate everyone on sight, or is it just me?'

She could make out the sensual line of his mouth, twisting in the moonlight.

'I know you. I've seen you... Plastered all over Paris on those posters. For months.'

Sylvie frowned. 'That was a year ago—when the new show opened.' *And that wasn't really me.* She'd been chosen for the photo shoot as she was more voluptuous than the other girls... but in truth she was the one who bared the least of all of them.

She knew she should pull back from this man, but she seemed to be unable to drum up the necessary motor skills to do so—and why wasn't he pushing her away? He was obviously one of those puritans who disapproved of women taking their clothes off in the name of entertainment.

His silent condemnation angered her even more.

She arched a brow. 'So that's it? Seeing me in the flesh has only confirmed your worst suspicions?'

She saw how his gaze dropped down between them, to where she could feel her breasts pressed against him. Her skin grew hot all over.

His voice sounded husky. 'Admittedly, there is a lot of flesh to see.' His gaze rose again and bored into hers. 'But then I guess not half as much as is usually on show.'

That ripped away the illusion of any cocoon. Sylvie tugged herself free of his grip and pushed against him to get away. She was too angry, though, not to give him a piece of her mind before she left.

'People like you make me sick. You judge and condemn and you've no idea what you're talking about.'

She took a step back towards him and stuck a finger in his chest, hating how aware she was of his innate masculinity.

'I'll have you know that the L'Amour revue is one of the most upmarket cabaret acts in the world. We are world-class trained dancers. It's not some seedy strip joint.'

His tone was dry. 'Yet you *do* take off your clothes?'

'Well...' The truth was that Sylvie's act didn't actually require her to strip completely. Her breasts were slightly too large, and Pierre preferred the flatter-chested girls to do the full nudity. It provided a better aesthetic, as far as he was concerned.

Arkim Al-Sahid emitted a sound of disgust. Sylvie wasn't sure if it was directed at her or himself.

And then he said, 'I couldn't care less if you stripped naked and hung upside down on a trapeze in your show. This conversation is over.'

Sylvie refrained from pointing out that that was actually Giselle's act, assuming he wouldn't appreciate it.

He'd turned and was stalking away before she could say anything more anyway, and Sylvie bubbled with futile indignation and hurt pride. And something else—something deeper. A need to not have him judge her so out of hand when his opinion shouldn't matter.

She blurted out the words before she could stop herself—an irritating side effect of her red hair: her temper. She hated being a cliché, but sometimes she couldn't help it.

He halted in his tracks, his broad frame silhouetted by the lights of the party and the house in the distance.

Slowly he turned around, incredulity visible on his face.

For a moment Sylvie had to choke back a semi-hysterical giggle, but then he said in an arctic tone, '*What* did you say?' and any urge to giggle died.

She refused to let herself be intimidated and drew back her shoulders. 'I believe I said that you are an arrogant, uptight prat.'

Arkim Al-Sahid prowled back towards her. Deep in the garden as they were, he was like a jungle cat, in spite of his still pristine three-piece suit. All predatory and menacing. There was a thrill in her blood that was extremely inappropriate as she found herself backing away... Until her back slammed into something solid. The gazebo.

He loomed over her now...larger than life. Larger than anyone she'd ever known. He caged her in with his hands either side of her head. Suddenly her heart was racing, her skin prickling with anticipation. His scent was exotic and musky. Full of dark promise and danger and wickedness.

'Are you going to apologise?'

Sylvie shook her head. 'No.'

For a long second he said nothing, and then, almost contemplatively, 'You're right, you know...'

Her breath stopped… Was he *apologising*? 'I am?'

He nodded slowly, and as he did so he lifted a hand and trailed one finger down over Sylvie's cheek and jaw to where the bare skin of her shoulder met her dress.

She was breathing so hard now she felt as if she might hyperventilate. Her skin was on fire where he touched her. *She* was on fire. No man had ever had this effect on her. It was overwhelming, and she was helpless to rationalise it.

'Yes,' he said in a low voice. 'I'm very *uptight*. All over. Maybe you could help me with that?'

Before she could react his arm had snaked around her waist, pulling her into him, and his other hand was deep in her hair, anchoring her head so that he could plunge his mouth down onto hers, stealing what little breath she had left along with her sanity.

It was like going from zero to one hundred in a nanosecond. This was no gentle, exploratory kiss. It was explicit and devastating. Sylvie's tongue was entwined with Arkim Al-Sahid's before the impulse to let him in had even registered. And there wasn't one part of her that rejected him—

which was so out of character for her that she couldn't appreciate the significance right now.

Her hands were on his chest, fingers curling into his waistcoat. Then they were climbing higher to curl around his neck, making her reach up on tip-toe to get closer.

Adrenalin and a kind of pleasure she'd never experienced before coursed through her blood. It radiated out from the core of her body and to every extremity, making her tingle and tighten with need.

His hand was on her dress now, at her shoulder, fingers tucking under the fabric, pulling it down.

There was something wild and earthy beating inside her as his mouth left hers and trailed down over her jaw, down to where her shoulder was now bare.

Sylvie's head tipped back, her eyes closed. Her entire world was reduced to this frantic, urgent beat that she had no will to deny as she felt her dress being pulled down, and cool night air drift-ing over hot skin.

Her head came up. She felt dizzy, drugged. 'Arkim...' She was dimly aware that she didn't even know this man. Yet here she was, entreating him to...to stop? Go on?

When he looked at her, though, those black eyes—like hard diamonds—robbed her of any ability to decide.

'Shh…let me touch you, Sylvie.'

His mouth wrapped around her name…it made her melt even more. His other hand was on her thigh, between them, inching up under her dress, pushing it up. This was more intimate than she'd ever been with any man, because she didn't let many get close, but it felt utterly right. Necessary. As if she'd been missing something her whole life and a key had just been slotted into place, unlocking some part of her.

Tacitly, her legs widened. She saw a glimmer of a smile on Arkim's face and it wasn't cruel, or judgemental. It was *sexy*.

He lowered his head to her now bared breast and closed his mouth over the pouting flesh, sucking her nipple deep and then rolling and flicking it with his tongue. Sylvie nearly shot into orbit. Electric shocks pulsed through her and tugged between her legs, where she was wet and aching…

And where Arkim's fingers were now exploring… Pushing aside her panties and sliding underneath, searching between slick folds and finding where her body gave him access, then thrusting a finger deep inside.

Sylvie's hands tightened, and it was only then that she realised she had them clasped on Arkim's head as his mouth suckled her and his finger moved in and out of her body, making a strange and new tension coil unbearably tight within her. Was this what he'd meant about being uptight? Because she felt it too. Deep in her core. Tightening so much it was almost unbearable.

Overcome with emotion at all the sensations rushing through her, she lifted Arkim's head from her breast, looking into those dark, fathomless eyes. 'I can't… What are you…?'

She couldn't speak. Could only feel. One minute she'd thought he was the devil incarnate, and now…now he was taking her to heaven. She was confused. His whole body was flush against hers, his leg pushing hers apart, his fingers exploring her so intimately…

Frustrated by her lack of ability to say anything, she leant forward and pressed her mouth to his again. But he went still. And then suddenly he was pulling away so fast Sylvie had to stop herself from falling forward. He stood back and looked at her as if she'd grown two heads, his horrified expression clear in the moonlight. His tie was askew and his waistcoat was undone. His hair mussed up. Cheeks flushed.

'What the hell…?'

Sylvie wanted to say, *My thoughts exactly*, but she was still struck mute.

Arkim backed away and said harshly, 'Don't *ever* come near me again.' And then he stalked off, back up the garden and into the light.

Three months ago…

Sylvie couldn't believe she was back at the house in Richmond again so soon. She usually managed to avoid it, because Sophie lived in central London in the family's *pied-à-terre*.

But the *pied-à-terre* wasn't suitable for this occasion: a party to celebrate the announcement of her little sister's engagement…to Arkim Al-Sahid.

Sylvie could still hear the shock in her sister's voice when she'd phoned her a few days ago: *'It's all happened so fast…'*

Nothing would have induced Sylvie to come into the bosom of her family again except for this. No way was she going to let her little sister be a pawn in her stepmother's machinations. Or *that* man's.

The man she'd been avoiding thinking about ever since that night. The man who had at first dismissed her and then... She shivered even now, her skin prickling with awareness at the thought of meeting him again.

The memory of what had happened was as sharp and humiliating as if it had happened yesterday. His voice. The disgust. *'Don't* ever *come near me again.'*

The shrill tones of Sylvie's stepmother hectoring some poor employee nearby stopped her thoughts from devolving rapidly into a kaleidoscope of unwelcome images.

Her hands closed over the rim of the sink in the bathroom as she took in her reflection.

Despite her best efforts she could still remember the excoriating wave of humiliation and exposure when she'd watched Arkim Al-Sahid walk away and realised that her breast was bared and her legs still splayed in wanton abandonment. Panties pulled aside. One shoe on, one off. And she'd been complicit—every step of the way. She couldn't even say he'd used force.

He'd crooked his finger and she'd all but come running. Panting. Practically begging.

The true magnitude of how easily she'd let

him—more or less a complete stranger—reduce her to a quivering wreck was utterly galling.

Sylvie cursed herself. She was here for Sophie—not to take a trip down memory lane. She stood up straight and checked her appearance. A far cry from the gold dress she'd worn that night. Now she was positively respectable, in a knee-length black sleeveless shift and matching high heels, her hair pulled back into a low bun. Discreet make-up.

She didn't like to think of the reaction in her body when her sister had informed her of the upcoming nuptials. It had been a mix of shock, incomprehension, anger—and something far more disturbing and dark.

Sylvie made her way into the huge dining room, which had been set up for a buffet-style dinner party. She was acutely aware of Arkim Al-Sahid, looking as grimly gorgeous as ever, and made sure to stay far away from him. It meant, though, that she couldn't get Sophie to herself. And she needed to talk to her.

The evening was interminable. Several times, as Sylvie made mind-numbingly boring small talk, she felt the back of her neck prickle—as if someone was staring at her...or more likely *glaring* at her. But each time she looked around she couldn't see him.

Not seeing her sister anywhere now, Sylvie determined to find her and went looking. The first place she thought to look was in her father's study/library, and she opened the door carefully, seeing nothing inside the oak-panelled room filled with heaving shelves of books but the fire, which was dying down low.

The warmth and peace called to her for a minute, and she slipped in and closed the door behind her.

Then she saw a movement coming from one of the high-backed chairs near the fire. 'Soph? Is that you?' The room had always been her little sister's favourite hiding place when she was younger, and Sylvie felt a lurch near her heart to think of her sister retreating here.

But it wasn't Sophie—which became apparent all too quickly when a tall, dark shape uncoiled from the chair to stand up.

Arkim Al-Sahid.

Instinctively Sylvie backed away, and said frigidly, 'At the risk of being accused of following you I can assure you I wasn't.' She turned to go, then stopped and turned back. 'Actually, I have something to say to you.'

He folded his arms. 'Do you, now?'

He was as implacable as a stone pillar. It infuriated Sylvie that he could so effortlessly arouse seething emotions within her. She stalked over to the chairs and gripped the back of the one he'd been sitting in. She hated it that he looked even more enigmatic and handsome. As if the intervening months had added more hard muscle to his form. Made his features even more saturnine.

He was dressed in similar pristine fashion to last time—in a three-piece suit. He sent a dismissive look up and down her body, and then said with a faint sneer, 'Who are you trying to fool? Or are we all going to be treated to an exclusive performance, in which you reveal the truth of what lies beneath your pseudo-respectable façade?'

Sylvie's anger spiked in a hot rush. 'At first I couldn't understand why you hated me on sight, but now I know. Your father is one of America's biggest porn barons, and you've made no secret of the fact that you disowned him *and* his legacy to forge your own. You don't even share his name any more.'

Arkim Al-Sahid's body vibrated with tension,

his dark eyes narrowing on her dangerously. 'As you said, it's no secret.'

'No...' Sylvie conceded, slightly thrown off balance by his response.

'And your point?'

She swallowed. Lord, but he was intimidating. Not a hint of humanity anywhere in his whipcord form or on that beautiful face.

'You're marrying my sister purely to gain social acceptance, and she deserves more than that. She deserves love.'

Arkim emitted a short, curt laugh. It was so shocking to see his face transformed by a smile—albeit a mocking one—that she almost lost her train of thought.

'You're for real? Since when does anyone marry for *love*? Your sister has a lot to gain from this union—not least a lifetime of security and status. At no point has she indicated that she's not happy for this engagement to proceed. Your father is keen to secure her future—which is no surprise, considering how his eldest daughter turned out.'

Sylvie kept her expression rigid. Amazing how this man's opinion sneaked under her guard with such devastating effect and struck far too close to the heart of her—which was the last place he should be impacting.

He continued. 'I'm not stupid, Miss Devereux. This is as much a business transaction for him as it is a chance to secure his daughter's future. It's not a secret that his empire took a big hit during the downturn and that he's doing all he can to bolster his coffers again.'

Business transaction. She felt nauseous. Sylvie knew vaguely that her father's fortune had taken a dip...but she also knew perfectly well that her stepmother was the real architect behind this plan. She was a firm believer that a woman's place was by her rich husband's side, and no doubt had convinced Grant Lewis that this was their ticket to security for the future.

She ungritted her teeth and desisted from belabouring the point of whether or not love existed. Clearly in his world it didn't.

'Sophie's not right for you—and you are certainly not right for *her.*'

An assessing look came over that starkly handsome face. 'She's perfect for me. Young, beautiful, intelligent. Accomplished.' He looked her up and down. 'And above all she's refined.'

Sylvie held up a hand, hating it that that stung.

'Please—save your insults. I'm perfectly aware where I come on your scale of condemnation. Clearly you have issues with certain industries, and you've deemed me worth judging on the basis of what I do.'

'What you *are*,' he said harshly.

Her hands clenched into fists. 'You didn't seem to have much of an issue with what I *am* the last time we met.'

His face flushed dark red and Sylvie felt the bite of his self-condemnation as sharply as if he'd just slapped her.

'That was a mistake—not to be repeated.'

Something about that lash of recrimination made her want to curl up and protect herself. The look on his face was pure…disgust. And it would have been worse if it was solely for her. But she could tell it wasn't. It was for himself.

Hurt lodged deep in her belly like a dark, malevolent thing, tugging on other hurts, reopening old wounds. Reminding her of the disgust on her father's face when he'd looked at her after her mother had died…

She desperately wanted to lash back and see this man's icy condemnatory control snap. Acting on blind instinct, and on that hurt, she stepped out from behind the chair and right up to Arkim Al-Sahid. She pressed her body to his, lifting her arms to wind them around his neck.

His nostrils flared and those black eyes flashed. His hands were on her arms, his grip tight. 'What the hell do you think you're doing?'

But he didn't pull her arms down. Sylvie's entire body was quivering with adrenalin at her bravado.

'I'm proving that you're a hypocrite, Mr Al-Sahid.'

And then, in the boldest move she'd ever made in her life, she reached up and pressed her mouth to his. She moved her lips over his and through the frantic thumping of her heart she could feel excitement flooding her at the sheer proximity of their bodies. Brain cells were scrambled in a rush of heat.

She could feel the tension holding his body rigid... But what he couldn't disguise was the explicit thrust of his arousal against her belly. That evidence was enough to send a thrill of exultation through Sylvie and help her block out the memory of how he'd pushed her away the last time.

Except then she started to forget why she'd even started this. Her body moved against him, closer. Arms locked tighter. And after a heart-stopping infinitesimal moment his hands loosened from her arms and slid down the length of her torso to her hips, gripping her there as his mouth started to move on hers—slowly at first and then, like a storm gathering strength, with an almost rough intensity.

For a long moment everything faded into the distance as the kiss became hotter and more intense. Arkim Al-Sahid's hands pulled Sylvie even closer—so close that she could feel his heart beating. And then something shifted. He went very still, before abruptly breaking the kiss.

Sylvie was left grasping air when he thrust her away from him. She stumbled backwards and found herself landing heavily in the chair behind her, her breathing laboured, her heart out of control. Dizzy.

Arkim's mouth twisted and his voice was rough. '*No.* I will not do this. You *dare* to try and seduce me on the evening of the announcement of my engagement to your sister? Is there no depth to which you won't descend?'

Sylvie was going cold all over. The lust which had risen up like wildfire dissipated under his murderous gaze. Her brain felt woolly...it was hard to think. Why had it been so important to kiss him like that? What had she been trying to prove? How did this man have the ability to make her act so out of character?

She looked up at him. 'It wasn't like that. I'd never do anything to hurt Sophie.'

Arkim made a rude sound just as a knock sounded at the door and it was opened.

Sylvie heard a voice say, 'Sorry to disturb you, Mr Al-Sahid, but they're ready to make the announcement.'

Sylvie realised that whoever was at the door wouldn't be able to see her in the chair just as Arkim Al-Sahid answered with a curt, 'I'll be right there.' The door closed again and he looked down at her, black eyes glittering with disgust and condemnation. 'I think it would be best for all of us if you left now, don't you?'

CHAPTER TWO

Present day—a week after the ruined wedding...

ARKIM AL-SAHID LOOKED out over the view from his palatial office and apartment complex, high in the London skyline. And even though the past week had brought to life a lot of his worst nightmares all he could think about right at that moment was of how he'd only met Sylvie Devereux twice in the past six months—three times if you counted her memorable appearance in the church—and yet each time he'd let his legendary control slip.

And now he was paying for it. More than he'd ever thought possible.

Anger was a constant unquenchable fire within him. He was paying for the fact that she was a privileged spoilt brat, who didn't take rejection well. Who had acted out of her poisonous jealousy of her younger sister to ruin their wedding.

Yet his conscience pricked him. It had been *him* who had fallen for her all too obvious charms. He'd had to fight it from the moment he'd laid eyes on her, when she'd stood in the reception hall of her father's house with her hand on her hip, her beautiful body flaunted to every best advantage.

He could still see her eyes landing on him, widening, the familiar glitter of feminine awareness, the scenting of his power. Sensing a conquest. And then she'd sashayed over as if she owned the world. As if she could own him with a mere flutter of her eyelids. And, dammit, he had almost fallen right then—as soon he'd seen those amazing eyes up close.

One blue and the other green and blue.

An intriguing genetic anomaly in a perfect face—high cheekbones, patrician nose and a mouth so lush it could incite a man to sin.

His body had come to hot, pulsing life under that knowing feline gaze, showing him that any illusion that he mastered his own impulses was just that: a flimsy illusion.

His mouth compressed now as he stared unseeingly out of the window, as if he could try to compress the memories.

The full repercussions of his weakness sat like

lead in his belly. The marriage to Sophie Lewis was off. And Arkim's very substantial investment in Grant Lewis's extensive industrial portfolio was teetering on the brink of collapse. Losing the deal wouldn't put much of a dent into Arkim's finances, but the subsequent loss of professional standing *would*.

He was back to square one. Having to prove himself all over again. His team had been fielding calls from clients all week, expressing doubts and fears that Arkim's solid business reputation was as shaky as his personal life. Stocks and shares were in freefall.

The tabloids had salivated over the story, featuring a caricaturised cast of characters: the stoical and long-suffering father; the scandalous daughter bent on revenge borne out of jealousy; the sweet innocent bride—the victim—and the ruthless social-climbing mother.

And Arkim—son of one of the world's richest men, who was also one of its most infamous, dominating the world's porn industry.

Saul Marks lived a life of excess in Los Angeles, and Arkim hadn't seen him since he was seventeen. He'd made a vow a long time ago to crawl out from under his father's shameful reputation, even going so far as to change his name legally as soon as he'd been able to—choosing a name that had belonged to a distant ancestor of his mother's as he hadn't thought her present-day immediate family would appreciate their bastard relative making a claim on their name.

Arkim's mother had come from a wealthy and high-born family in the Arabian country of Al-Omar. She'd been studying in the States at university when she'd met and been seduced by Saul Marks. Naive and innocent, she'd been bowled over by the handsome charismatic American.

When she'd become pregnant, however, Marks had already moved on to his next girlfriend. He'd supported Arkim's mother, but wanted nothing to do with her or the baby…until she'd died in childbirth and he'd been forced to take his baby son into his care after Zara's family in Al-Omar had expressed no interest in their deceased daughter's son.

Arkim's early life had been a constant round of English boarding schools and impersonal nannies, interspersed with time spent with a reluctant father and his dizzying conveyer belt of lovers, who invariably came from the porn industry. One of whom had taken an unhealthy interest in Arkim and given him an important life lesson in how vital it was to master self-control.

But a week ago, when the society wedding of the decade had imploded in scandalous fashion, all those ambitions and his efforts to distance himself from shame and scandal had turned to dust.

And all because of a red-haired witch.

A witch who had somehow managed to sneak under his impenetrable guard. It was galling to recall how hard it had been to let her go that night in the study. How hard *he'd* been. From the moment he'd first seen her appear. Looking like a schoolteacher. With her hair pulled back, her face pale. Covered up.

He'd only come to his senses because there had been something in the way she'd kissed him—something he hadn't believed... Something innocent. Gauche. But it was a lie—as if she'd been trying to figure out what he liked. Acting sweet and innocent after she'd just been completely brazen. Attempting to seduce him away from her sister.

The only thing that had got Arkim through the past week of ignominy and public embarrassment had been the prospect of making Sylvie Devereux pay. And the kind of payment he had in mind would finally exorcise her from his head, and his body, once and for all.

For months she'd inhabited the dark, secret corners of his mind and his imagination. She'd been the cause of sleepless nights and lurid dreams. Even during his engagement to her far sweeter and infinitely more innocent sister.

Apart from the injury Sylvie had caused to Arkim with her selfish behaviour, she'd also recklessly played with her sister's life. The young woman had been inconsolable, absolutely adamant that she wouldn't give Arkim another chance. And could he blame her? Who would believe the son of a man who lived his life as if it was a bacchanal?

The words Sylvie Devereux had said in the church still rang in his head: *'This man shared my bed.'* And yet even now his body reacted to those words with a surge of frustration. Because she most certainly had *not* shared his bed. It had been a bare-faced lie. Conjured up to create maximum damage.

Sylvie Devereux wanted him so badly? Well, then, she'd have him—until he was sated and he could throw her back in the trash, where she belonged.

But it would be on *his* terms, and far out of the

reach of the ravenous public's gaze. The damage to his reputation stopped right here.

Sylvie looked out of the small private plane's window to see a vast sea of sand below her, and in the distance, shimmering in a heat haze, a steel city that might have come directly from a futuristic movie.

The desert sands of Al-Omar and its capital city, B'harani.

Some called it the jewel of the Middle East. It was one of its most progressive countries, presided over by a very dynamic and modern royal couple. Sylvie had just been reading an article about them in the in-flight magazine: Sultan Sadiq and his wife Queen Samia, and their two small cherubic children.

Queen Samia was younger than Sylvie, and she'd felt a little jaded, looking at the beaming smile on the woman's face. She was pretty, more than beautiful, and yet her husband looked at her as if he'd never seen a woman before.

She'd seen her father look at her mother like that.

Sylvie ruthlessly crushed the small secret part of her that clenched with an ominous yearning.

The cynicism she'd honed over years came to the fore. Sultan Sadiq might well be reformed now, but she could remember when he'd been a regular visitor to the infamous L'Amour revue and had cut a swathe through some of its top-billed stars.

Not Sylvie, though. Once she was offstage and dressed down, with her hair tied back, she slipped unnoticed past all her far more glamorous peers. She courted endless teasing from the other girls—and from the guys, who were mostly gay—having earned the moniker of 'Sister Sylvie', because of the way she would prefer to go home and curl up with a book or cook a meal rather than head out to party with their inevitably rich and gorgeous clientele. A clientele that appreciated the very discreet ethos of the revue *and* any liaisons that ensued out of hours.

But even they—her friends, who were more like her family now—didn't know the full extent of her duality...how far from her stage persona she really was.

'Miss Devereux? We'll be landing shortly.'

Sylvie looked up at the beautiful olive-skinned stewardess, with her dark brown eyes and glossy black hair. She forced a smile, suddenly reminded of someone with similar colouring. Someone infinitely more masculine, though, and more dangerous than this courteous flight attendant.

That fateful day almost two weeks ago rushed back with a garish vividness that took her breath away. Reminding her painfully of the searing public scrutiny, judgement and humiliation. And *his* face. So dark and unforgiving. Those black eyes scorching the skin from her body.

He'd moved towards her, his anger palpable. But her stepmother had reached her first, slapping Sylvie so hard that her teeth had rattled in her head and the corner of her lip had split. It was still tender when she touched her tongue to it now.

And then she saw in her mind's eye her sister's face. Pale and tear-streaked. Eyes huge. Shocked. *Relieved.* That relief had made it all worthwhile. Sylvie didn't regret what she'd done for a second. Sophie hadn't been right for Arkim Al-Sahid.

Her feeling of vindication had been fleeting, though. The truth was, when she'd stood behind them in that church her motivation for stopping the wedding had felt far more complex than it should have.

Arkim was the only man who'd managed to breach the defences Sylvie hadn't even been aware she'd erected so high. She'd bared herself to him

in a way she'd never done with anyone else—
which was ironic, considering her profession—
only to be cruelly pushed aside...as if she was a
piece of dirt on his shoe. Not worthy to look him
in the eye.

But her sister *was* worthy. Her beautiful blonde,
sweet sister. Just as Sophie was worthy of their father's affections. Because *she* didn't remind him
of his beloved dead first wife.

Maybe it was this stark landscape that was making her think about all of that—and *him*. Forcing
him up into her consciousness. She buckled her
seat belt, diverting her mind away from painful
memories and towards what lay ahead. The problem was that she wasn't even entirely sure what
lay ahead.

She and some of the other girls from the revue
had been invited over to put on a private show for
an important sheikh's birthday celebrations. Sylvie wasn't flying with the others because they'd
travelled before her. She'd only been asked to join
them afterwards—hence her solo trip on the private jet.

It wasn't unusual for this kind of thing to happen. Their revue had performed privately for
A-list stars around the world, much as a pop star

might be asked to perform, and they'd done a residency one summer in Las Vegas. But this... Something about this made Sylvie's skin prickle uncomfortably.

She tried to reassure herself that she was being silly. The other girls would be waiting for her, they'd rehearse and perform, and then they'd be home before they knew it.

They were landing now, and she noticed that they were quite far outside the city limits, with nothing but desert as far as the eye could see. The airport didn't look like a busy capital city's airport. Just a few small buildings and a runway carved into the arid landscape. She pushed the nervous flutters down.

Once the small jet had taxied to a gentle stop Sylvie was escorted to the door of the plane—and the heat of the desert hit her so squarely that she had to suck in a breath of hot, dry air. Sweat instantly dampened the skin all over her body. But along with the trepidation she felt at what lay ahead was a quickening of something like exhilaration as she took in the clear blue vastness of the sky and the rolling dunes in the distance.

She was so far away from everything that was familiar in this completely alien landscape, but it soothed her a little after the last tumultuous couple of weeks. It was as if nothing here could hurt her.

'Miss, your car is waiting.'

Sylvie looked down to see a sleek black car. She put on her sunglasses and went down the steps and across the scorching runway to where a driver was holding the back door open. He was dressed in a long cream tunic, with close-fitting trousers underneath and a turban on his head. He looked smart and cool, and she felt ridiculously under-dressed in her jeans, ballet flats and loose T-shirt. Like a gauche westerner.

Someone was putting her cases into the boot, and Sylvie smiled as the driver bowed deferentially, indicating for her to get in.

She did so—with relief. Already craving the cool balm of air-conditioning. Already wanting to twist her long, heavy hair up and off her neck.

The door was closed quickly behind her and then a lot of things seemed to happen simultaneously: she heard the snick of the door locking, the driver slid into the front seat and the privacy partition slid up, and Sylvie realised that she wasn't alone in the back of the car.

'I trust you had a pleasant flight?'

The voice was deep, cool—and instantly, painfully, recognisable. Sylvie turned her head and everything seemed to go into slow motion.

Arkim Al-Sahid was sitting at the far side of the luxurious car, which was now moving. A fact she was only vaguely aware of. She went hot and cold all at once. Her belly dropped near her feet. Her breath was caught in her chest. Shock was seizing at her ability to respond.

He was dressed in his signature three-piece suit. As if they were in Paris or London. En route to some civilised place. Not here, in the middle of a harsh sun-beaten land. Here in the middle of nowhere. Here where she'd just thought nothing could touch her.

Arkim Al-Sahid looked so dark, and his face was etched in lines of cruelty.

A small voice jeered at Sylvie, *Did you really think he would do nothing?* And underneath the shock was the pounding of her heart that told her that perhaps, in some very deep and hidden secret space, she *hadn't* thought he would do nothing. But she'd never expected this…

He reached forward and her sunglasses were plucked off her face and tucked away into his pocket before she could react. She blinked, and he came into sharp, clear focus. Dark hair brushed back from a high forehead. Deep-set eyes over sharp cheekbones. His patrician nose giving him a slightly hawk-like aspect.

And that mouth… That cruel and taunting mouth. The mouth that even now she could recall being on hers. Hard and demanding, sending her senses into overdrive. It was curved up into the semblance of a smile, but it was a smile unlike anything Sylvie had ever seen. It was a smile that promised retribution.

When she remained mute with shock, one dark brow arched up lazily. 'Well, Sylvie? I'll be exceedingly disappointed over the next two weeks if you've lost the ability to do anything with your tongue.'

Arkim tried to ignore the frantic rate of his pulse, which had burst to life as soon as he'd seen her distinctive shape appear in the doorway of the plane. Slim, yet womanly. Even in casual clothes.

Her glorious red hair glowed like the setting sun over the Arabian sea. Her face was as pale as alabaster, her skin perfect and flawless. Her eyes were huge and almond-shaped, giving her that feline quality, her left eye with that distinctive discolouration. It did nothing to diminish her appeal—it only enhanced it.

Irritation rose at her effortless ability to control his libido.

Arkim was about to say something else when she got out a little threadily, 'Where are the other girls?'

He felt a twinge of guilt, but pushed it down deep. He glanced briefly at his watch. 'They're most likely performing, as arranged, for the birthday celebrations of one of the Sultan's chief advisors—Sheikh Abdel Al-Hani. They'll be on a plane first thing tomorrow morning.'

If possible, Sylvie paled even more. It sent a jolt of something horribly like concern through him, reminding him of when her stepmother had slapped her in the church and how his first instinctive reaction had been to put himself between them. *Not* something he relished remembering now.

But now the shocked glaze was leaving her face, colour was surging back into her cheeks and her eyes were sparking. 'So why am I not there too? What the hell *is* this, Arkim?'

Nurturing the sense of satisfaction at having Sylvie where he wanted her, rather than his other more tangled emotions, Arkim settled back into his seat. 'Believe it or not, people here call me Sheikh too—a title conferred upon me by the Sultan himself...an old schoolfriend. But I digress. This is about payback. It's about the fact that your jealous little tantrum had far-reaching consequences and you aren't going to get away with it.'

Sylvie put out a hand and Arkim noticed it was trembling slightly. He ruthlessly pushed down his concern. Again. This woman didn't deserve anything but his scorn.

'So...what? You're kidnapping me?'

Arkim picked a piece of lint off his jacket and then looked at her. 'I'd call it a...a *holiday*. You came here of your own free will and you're free to go at any time... It's just not going to be that easy for you to leave when there's no public transport and no mobile phone coverage, so I'm afraid you'll have to wait until I'm leaving too. In two weeks.'

Sylvie clenched her hands into fists on her lap, her jaw tight. 'I'll damn well walk across the desert if I have to.'

Arkim was calm. 'Try it and you'll be lucky to last twenty-four hours. It's certain death for anyone who doesn't know the lie of this land—not to mention the fact that someone as fair as you would fry to a crisp.'

Sylvie was reeling, and trying hard not to show it. She felt as if she'd fallen through a wormhole and everything was upside down and inside out. Panic tightened her gut.

'What about my job? I'm expected back—it was only supposed to be a one-night event.'

Arkim's face was scarily expressionless. It made her want to reach across and slap him, to see some kind of reaction.

'Your job is unaffected. Your boss has been recompensed very generously for the use of your time. So much so, in fact, that I believe he can finally start the renovations he's been wanting to do for years. As a result of my generous donation the revue is actually closing for a month from next week, while they do the work.'

She had to choke back a lurch of even greater panic; it was common knowledge how much Pierre wanted to renovate—he'd been begging for loans from banks for months. And this would be perfect timing...before the high tourist season.

She spluttered. 'Pierre would never let one of his girls go off on an assignment alone. He'll raise hell when I don't return, no matter how much you've offered him!'

Arkim smiled, and it was cold. 'Pierre is like anyone else in this world—mesmerised when large sums of money are mentioned. He's been assured that your services are required as dance teacher to one of the Sheikh's daughters and her friends, who want to learn the western way of dancing. The fact that you're here with me instead is something he doesn't need to be aware of.'

Sylvie folded her arms, trying to not let on how scared she was. She injected mockery into her voice. 'I'm surprised. I would have thought your morals wouldn't allow you to come within ten feet of me—much less arrange a private performance.'

Arkim was no longer smiling. 'I'm prepared to risk a little moral corruption for what I want—and I want you.'

She sucked in a breath at hearing him declare it so baldly. 'I should have known you'd have no scruples. So you've effectively *bought* me? Like some kind of call girl?'

Arkim's mouth curled up into that cruel smile again. 'Come now…we both know that that's not so far from the truth of what you are.'

This time Sylvie couldn't hold back. She was

across the seat and launching herself at Arkim, hand outstretched, ready to strike, when he caught her wrists in his hands. They were like steel manacles, and she fell heavily against his body.

Instantly awareness sparked to life, infusing her veins with heat and electricity. Even now, when she was in the grip of panic and anger.

'Let me *go*.'

Arkim's jaw was like granite, and this close she could see the depths of anger banked deep in his eyes. He was livid. She felt a quiver of real fear— even though, perversely, she knew he wouldn't hurt her physically.

'No way. We have unfinished business and we're not leaving this place until it's done.'

Sylvie was excruciatingly aware of her body, pressed to Arkim's much harder and more powerful one. Of the way her breasts were crushed against him, as they'd been crushed against him once before…when he'd thrust her back from him and looked at her as if she'd given him a contagious disease.

'What are you talking about?' she asked, hating the tremor in her voice.

The expression in his eyes changed for the first

time, flashing with a heat that Sylvie felt deep in her belly.

'What I'm talking about is the fact that I'm going to have you—over and over again—for however long it takes until I can think straight again.' A note of unmistakable bitterness entered his voice. 'You've done it, Sylvie—you've got me.'

She finally broke free from Arkim's grip and sat back, as far away as she could. 'I don't want you.' *Liar*, whispered an inner voice. She ignored it. She hated Arkim Al-Sahid. 'As soon as this car stops I'm out of here, and you can't stop me.'

Arkim merely looked amused. 'Each time we've met you've demonstrated how much you want me, so protesting otherwise won't work now. Where we're going has no public transport, and it would take you about a week to walk to B'harani—days in any other direction before you hit civilisation.'

Sylvie crossed her arms over her chest, a feeling of claustrophobia threatening to strangle her. 'This is ridiculous.' The thought of being alone with this man in some remote desert for the next two weeks was overwhelming. 'You can't force me to do anything I don't want to do, you know.'

He looked at her, and there was something so explicit in his gaze that she felt herself blushing.

'I won't need to use force, Sylvie.'

And just like that the humiliation she'd felt that night in the study of her father's house came back and rolled over her like a wave.

She fought it. 'This just proves how little you really felt for my sister. Hurting me will only hurt *her*.'

The expression on Arkim's face became incredulous at the mention of Sophie 'You *dare* speak to me of hurting your sister? When *you* were the one who callously humiliated her in public?'

Words of defence trembled on Sylvie's tongue, but she bit them back. She would never betray her sister's confidence. Sophie had just been a pawn to him. It never would have worked. She had to remember that. She'd done the right thing.

But then she saw something in the distance and became distracted.

Arkim followed her gaze and said, 'Ah, we're here.'

Here was another, even smaller airfield, with a sleek black helicopter standing ready.

Slightly hysterically Sylvie remembered something she'd learnt when she'd taken self-defence classes after a—luckily—minor mugging in Paris. The tutor had told the class the importance of not letting an attacker take you to another location at all costs. Because if he did get you to another place, then your chances of survival were dramatically cut down.

It would appear to be common sense, but the tutor had told them numerous stories of people who had been so frightened they'd just let themselves be taken to another place, when they should always have tried to get away during the initial attack.

And okay, so technically Arkim wasn't attacking Sylvie, but she knew that if she got into that helicopter her chances of emerging from this encounter unscathed were nil.

The car came to a stop and he looked at her. 'Time to go.'

Sylvie shook her head. 'I'm not getting out. I'm staying in this car and it's going to take me back to wherever we landed. Or to B'harani. I hear it's a nice city—I'd like to visit.'

She hoped the desperation she was feeling wasn't evident.

He turned to face her more fully. 'This car is driven by a man who speaks only one language, and it's not yours. He answers to me—no one else.'

The sheer hardness of Arkim's expression told

her she was on a hiding to nothing. A sense of futility washed over her. She wouldn't win this round.

'Where is it that you're proposing to take me?'

'It's a house I own on the Arabian coast. North of B'harani and one hundred miles from the border of Burquat. Merkazad is in a westerly direction, about six hundred miles.'

The geographical details somehow made Sylvie feel calmer, even though she still had no real clue where they were. She'd heard of these places, but never been.

Something occurred to her. 'This…' her mouth twisted '…this fee you've paid Pierre. I assume it's conditional on my agreeing to this farcical non-existent dance tuition?'

Arkim nodded. 'That's good business sense, I think you'll agree.'

Sylvie wanted to tell him where he could stick his business sense, but she refrained. She didn't doubt that there really was no option but to go with Arkim. For now.

'Once we're at this…this place, you won't force me to do anything I don't want to?'

Arkim shook his head, eyes gleaming with a

disturbing light. 'No, Sylvie. There will be no force involved. I'm not into sadism.'

His smug arrogance made her want to try and slap him again. Instead, she sent him a wide, sunny, smile. 'You know, work has been so crazy busy lately I'm actually looking forward to an all-expenses-paid break. The fact that I have to share space with *you* is unfortunate, but I'm sure we can stay out of each other's way.'

Arkim just smiled slowly, and with an air of sensual menace, as if he knew just how flimsy her bravado was.

'We'll see.'

Sylvie had never been in a helicopter before, and she'd been more mesmerised than she cared to admit by the way the desert dunes had unfolded beneath them, undulating into the distance like the sinuous curves of a body. It all seemed utterly foreign and yet captivating to her.

Her stomach was only just beginning to climb back down from her throat when she heard a deep voice in her ear through the headphones.

'That's my house, Al-Hibiz, directly down and to your left.'

Sylvie looked down and her breath was taken

away. *House?* This was no house. It looked like a small but formidable castle, complete with ramparts and flat roofs. It was distinctly Arabic in style, with ochre-coloured walls. Within those walls she could see lush gardens, and in the distance the Arabian sea sparkled. What looked like an oasis lay far off in the distance, a spot of deep green. It was like something out of a fairytale.

It distracted her from the shock she still felt after realising that Arkim was co-piloting the helicopter, and the way his hands had lingered as he'd strapped her in, those fingers resting far too close to her breasts under her thin T-shirt.

He should have looked ridiculous, getting into the cockpit still dressed in his suit, against the backdrop of the stark desert, but he hadn't. He'd looked completely at home, powerful and utterly in control.

And now the helicopter was descending onto a flat area just outside the walls of the castle, which looked much bigger from this vantage point.

Sylvie could see robed men waiting, holding on to their long garments and the turbans on their heads as the helicopter kicked up sand and wind. When the craft bounced gently onto the earth she breathed out a deep sigh of relief, unaware of how tense she'd been.

The helicopter blades stopped turning and a delicious silence settled over them for a moment, before Arkim got out and the men approached. She watched as he greeted the men heartily in a guttural language that still managed to sound melodic, a wide smile on his face.

It took her breath away. It was the first genuine smile she'd ever seen on his face. Admittedly their previous encounters hadn't exactly been conducive to such a reaction. Not unless she counted that sexy smile when his hand had explored between her legs—

'Time to get out, Sylvie. I'm afraid the chopper has to go back and you're not going to be in it.'

She scowled, hating to be caught out in such a memory. She fumbled with the seat belt and swatted his hand away when he would have helped. Eventually it came undone and she extricated her arms, unaware of how the movement pulled her T-shirt taut over her breasts, or of how Arkim's dark gaze settled there for a moment with a flash of hunger. If she'd seen that she might well have barricaded herself into the helicopter, come hell or high water.

But then she was out, and swaying a little unsteadily on the firm sun-baked ground.

Staff dressed in white rushed to and fro, loading luggage into the back of a small people carrier, and then Arkim was leading Sylvie over to what looked like a luxurious golf buggy. He indicated for her to get in, and after a moment's futile rebellion she did so.

She really was stuck here now—with him.

He got in beside her and drove the small open-sided vehicle to the entrance of the castle, where huge wooden doors were standing open. They entered a beautiful airy courtyard, with a fountain in the centre. A deliciously cool gentle mist of moisture settled on her skin from the spray.

But the vehicle had stopped now, and Arkim was at her side, holding out a hand. Sylvie ignored it and stepped out, not wanting to see what would undoubtedly be a mocking look on his face.

When he didn't move, though, she had to look at him. He gestured with a hand and—damn him—a mocking smile.

'Welcome to my home, Sylvie. I expect our time here to be...cathartic.'

CHAPTER THREE

SYLVIE PACED BACK and forth in the rooms she'd been shown to by Arkim. *Cathartic! The arrogant, patronising son-of-a—*

A knock sounded on the door and she halted, her breathing erratic. Her hands balled into fists at her sides—she wasn't ready to see Arkim again.

Cautiously she approached the ornately decorated door and opened it, ready to do battle, only to find two pretty, smiling women on the other side. They had her two wheelie suitcases. One filled with now redundant dance costumes, the other with her own clothes.

She forced a smile and stood back. They entered meekly and she observed their pristine white dresses. Like long tunics. They wore white head coverings too, but not veils obscuring their faces. They looked cool and fresh, and Sylvie felt sticky and gritty after the tumultuous day.

As they were leaving again one of the girls stopped and said shyly, 'I'm Halima. If you need anything just pick up the phone and I will come to you.'

She ducked her head and then was gone, leaving Sylvie feeling a little slack-jawed. She had her own *maid*?

Arkim had left her here with a curt instruction to rest and said that he'd let her know when dinner would be ready. Sylvie could see the sky outside turning blood-red from the setting sun, and for the first time took in the sheer opulence of the rooms.

She was in a reception area that would have housed her small Parisian apartment three times over. It was a huge octagonal space, with a small pond in the centre with a tiled bottom and sides, where exotic fish swam lazily.

There were eight rooms off this main area. Two guest bedrooms, a dining room, and a living room complete with state-of-the-art sound system and media centre which had had all channels available when Sylvie had flicked it on.

The decor throughout was subtle and understated. The stone walls of the castle had been left exposed. and modern artwork and an eclectic mix of antiques enhanced the rather austere ancient building. Huge oriental rugs adorned the floors, softening any sharp edges further. The windows were all open to the elements, and even though it was sweltering outside, the castle had been designed so that balmy breezes wafted through the open rooms.

There was also a gym, and an accompanying thermal suite with hot-tub and sauna/steam room. And then there was the main bedroom suite, dressed in tones of dark red and cream. A fan circled overhead, distributing the air to keep it cool.

She'd never considered herself much of a sensualist, beyond tapping into her inner performer for her work, but right now her senses were heightened by everything she'd seen since she'd arrived in this country.

The bed was situated in the middle of the room, and strewn with opulent coverings and pillows. It had four posters and luxurious drapes, which were held back in place by delicately engraved gold curtain ties. The bed looked big enough to hold a football team with room to spare, let alone one person... *Or two*, inserted a snide voice, which Sylvie ignored.

One thing she was sure of: Arkim Al-Sahid would *not* be sharing her bed. Yet something quivered to life deep inside her and she couldn't seem to take her eyes off it…an image filled her brain of naked pale limbs entwined with much darker ones.

For years Sylvie had seen her peers indulge in casual sexual relationships and on some level had envied them that ease and freedom. She'd gone on dates…but the men involved had all expected her to be something she wasn't. And when they'd pushed for intimacy she'd found herself shutting down. The prospect that they'd somehow 'see' the real her and reject her was a fear she couldn't shake.

It was galling that she seemed to be hardwired to want more than casual sex—based on a fragile memory of the happiness and joy that had existed between her parents before her mother had so tragically died. She'd somehow clung to it her whole life, letting it sink deep into her unconscious.

It was even more galling, though, that Arkim Al-Sahid could look at her with explicit intent and have the opposite effect from making her shut down. When he looked at her she felt as if something was flowering to life deep inside her.

Irritated with the direction of her thoughts, and telling herself she was being ridiculous, Sylvie walked over to the French doors of the main bed-room and stepped outside. Heat washed over her like a dry caress, sinking into her bones and melting some of the tension away in spite of her wish to stay rigid at all costs.

She had her own private terrace, complete with a sparkling lap pool, its turquoise tiles illuminating the water. Low seats were scattered in twos and threes around low tables, with soft raw silk cushions. Lanterns hung from the walls, but weren't lit. Sylvie could imagine how seductive it might be at night, with only the flickering lights and the vast expanse of a star-filled night sky surrounding her.

And then she berated herself for getting sucked into a daydream so easily. Pushing the images out of her head, she walked over to the boundary wall, with its distinctive Arabic carvings. Outside she could see nothing but desert and dunes. A bird of prey circled lazily against the intense blue of the sky.

It compounded her sense of isolation and entrapment, and yet...much to her chagrin...Sylvie couldn't seem to drum up any sense of urgency. She realised that she was exhausted from the shock and adrenalin of the day.

A sound made her whirl around from the wall, her heart leaping into her throat. But it was only Halima again, with her shy smile.

'Sheikh Al-Sahid has sent me to tell you that he would be happy for you to join him in an hour for dinner. He said that should give you time to freshen up.'

Sylvie felt grim. 'Did he, now?' She thought of something and said, 'Wait here a moment—I'd like you to give him something, please.'

When she came back she felt unaccountably lighter. She handed the girl a folded-up note and said sweetly, 'Please give this to Sheikh Al-Sahid for me.'

The girl scurried off and Sylvie closed the door. A wave of weariness came over her, dousing any small sense of rebellious triumph. She set about unpacking only the most necessary items from her case, having no intention of staying here beyond a night. Whatever she had to do to persuade Arkim to let her go, she'd do it.

She was disappointed but unsurprised to see that her mobile phone didn't work. Exactly as he'd told her. She put it down and sighed, then took off her clothes, finding a robe. When she got to the door leading into the bathroom she had to suck in a breath. The sinks and the bath seemed to be carved out of the stone itself, with gold fittings that managed to complement the stark design without being tacky.

The bath was more like a small pool. When she'd filled it up, and added some oils she'd found in a cleverly hidden cabinet, exotically fragrant steam wrapped around her in a caress.

She drew off the robe and took the few steps down into the bath, trying not to feel too overwhelmed by the sheer luxury. The water closed over her body and as she tipped her head back she closed her eyes and pushed all thoughts of Arkim Al-Sahid out of her mind, trying to pretend she was on a luxury mini-break and not in the middle of an unforgiving desert, cut off from civilisation with someone who hated her guts.

Arkim stood looking out over the view, at the fading twilight casting the dunes into mysterious shadows. He had claimed this part of his maternal ancestral home for himself. His mother's family had no interest in him, and he'd told himself a long time ago that he didn't care. They'd rejected her and he wanted nothing to do with them—even if they came begging.

He'd come here initially as an exercise in removing himself from his father's sphere. He'd never expected this land to touch him as deeply as it had done on first sight. Almost with a physical pull. His mind automatically felt freer, less constrained, when he was here. He felt connected with something primal and visceral.

When he'd made his first million this property had been his first purchase, and he'd followed it up with properties in Paris, London and New York. He'd surpassed his goals one by one. All of them. Only to fall at the last hurdle: gaining the stamp of social approval and respect that would show everyone that he was *not* his father's son. That he was vastly different.

He thought of Sophie Lewis now and his conscience twinged. He hadn't thought of her very often. In truth, he'd had his doubts—their relationship had been very...platonic. But Arkim had convinced himself that it suited him like that. Her father had been the one to suggest the match, and the more Arkim had thought about it the more the idea had grown on him.

In contrast to her flame-haired provocative sister, Sophie had been like a gentle balm. Shy and innocent. Arousing no hormone-fuelled lapses of character. He'd courted her. Taken her for dinner. To the theatre. Each outing had soothed another piece of his wounded soul, making him believe that marriage to her would indeed offer him everything he'd ever wanted—which was the antithesis of life with his father.

He would be one of those parents who was respectable—respected—who came to school to pick up his son with his beautiful wife by his side. A united front. There would be no scandals. No children born out of wedlock. No mistresses. No sordid rumours and sniggering behind his back. No child of *his* would have to deal with bullying and fist fights when another kid taunted him about the whores his father took to his bed.

But the gods had laughed in his face at his ambitions and shown him that he was a fool to believe he could ever remove the stain of his father's legacy from his life.

He looked at the crumpled piece of paper in his hand and opened it out again to read.

Thank you for the kind 'invitation' to dinner, but I must decline. I've already made plans for this evening.
Sincerely, Sylvie Devereux.

Arkim had to battle both irritation and the lust that had held his body in an uncomfortable grip since he'd seen Sylvie earlier that day. He fought the urge to go straight to her room to confront her. No doubt that was exactly what she wanted.

He'd annoyed her by bringing her here and she was toying with him to get her own back. His mouth tipped up in a hard smile. No matter. He didn't mind being toyed with as long as she ended up where he wanted her—underneath him, naked and pliant and begging for mercy. Begging forgiveness.

When Sylvie woke it was dawn outside. She felt as if she'd slept for a week, not just the ten or so hours she *had* slept. Strangely, there was no disorientation—she knew exactly where she was.

She was still in the robe and she sat up, looking around warily, as if she might find Arkim lurking in a corner, glaring at her. She wondered how he'd reacted when she hadn't shown for dinner. She wasn't sure she wanted to know...

She got up and opened the French doors, the early morning's cool breeze a balm compared to the stifling heat which would no doubt come once the sun was up. She walked to the boundary wall again and sucked in a deep breath. The intense silence wrapped around her. She couldn't remember the last time she'd experienced this level of stillness—if ever. It seemed to quiet something inside her...some sense of restlessness. It was disconcerting—as if she was betraying herself by finding an affinity with any part of this situation.

She went back inside and dressed in jeans and a clean T-shirt, loath to make any kind of effort with clothes or to leave her rooms in case it showed acquiescence to Arkim. But she was also feeling somewhat trapped, and she didn't like it.

In the end Halima appeared, fresh-faced and smiling, with a tray of breakfast, bringing it into the dining room.

Sylvie's stomach rumbled loudly and she realised that because she'd turned down dinner the previous evening she'd not eaten since she'd been on the plane the day before. She was starving, and when Halima pulled back a cloth napkin to reveal a plate of fragrant flat breads Sylvie had to bite back of a groan of appreciation. It was a mezze-style feast, with little bowls of olives and different cheeses, hard and soft. And a choice of fragrant coffee or sweet tea.

Before she left, Halima said, 'Sheikh Al-Sahid

sends his apologies. He's been detained by a business call otherwise he would have joined you. He said he will meet you for lunch.'

Sylvie forced a smile. She couldn't shoot the messenger. 'Thank you.'

After Halima left and Sylvie had eaten her fill, she wandered around her rooms for a bit, feeling increasingly claustrophobic. She knew she should really do some exercises to keep herself flexible, especially after travelling, but she was feeling too antsy to focus. She left her rooms and walked down long stone corridors that gave glimpses into intriguing courtyards and other open spaces.

Through one open courtyard she saw a terrace with tall ornate stone columns and a vast pool that stretched around the side of the castle. It was breathtaking. Idyllic.

Sylvie backed away from the seductive scene and explored further. Some doors were closed, and she refrained from opening them in case she stumbled into Arkim.

Eventually she found herself at the main door, which led out to the central courtyard. Adrenalin flooded her system when she saw the golf buggy that Arkim had used to bring them into the castle the previous day. The key was in the ignition.

And from here she could see that the main doors to the castle complex were open.

She had a sudden vision of Arkim wearing down her defences, slowly but surely. If he kissed her again she was very much afraid that she'd melt—just as she had before, when she'd lost all control of her rational functions.

The truth was that she didn't have an arsenal of experience to fend off someone like Arkim, and the thought of him ever discovering how flimsy her façade was made her go cold with terror.

She didn't think. She reacted. She got into the golf buggy and turned the key, setting it in motion. Her heart was clamouring as she sped out of the castle complex.

Less than an hour later Sylvie's feet sank into the sand. She was on top of a dune, with the now dead golf buggy in front of her. Futile anger made her kick ineffectually at the inanimate object. It had started sputtering and slowing down about ten minutes before, eventually conking out.

The sun beat down mercilessly and there was nothing as far as the eye could see except sand, sand and more sand. Heat waves shimmered in the distance.

Of course it was only now that Sylvie realised just how stupid she'd been to react to her own imagination like that and set off in a panic. She had no water. No food. No idea where she was. Even if she'd had the means she wasn't sure which way she'd come!

Her T-shirt was stuck to her skin and her jeans felt red-hot and too tight. Right now she would have given anything for a cool white tunic and a head-covering. She could feel her skin prickling uncomfortably under the sun, and the roof of the buggy offered scant protection.

She gulped and, absurdly, tears pricked her eyes. Arkim Al-Sahid had driven her to this desperate measure. She wished she'd never laid eyes on the man. She wished he'd never kissed—

Something caught at her peripheral vision and she looked. For a second she wondered if she was seeing things, and then as the image became more distinct her eyes widened.

It was a man on top of a horse… Except this looked like no ordinary horse. It was a huge black stallion. And the man…

Sylvie felt as if she might have slipped back a few centuries. At first she thought it must be one of Arkim's staff, because he was dressed in white robes, with a *keffiyeh* around his head. His face was obscured by the material, leaving only his eyes and dark skin visible. And was that a jewelled dagger stuck into the roped belt around his waist?

He drew up alongside her, the horse rearing up, making Sylvie back away skittishly. Even now—even though her accelerated pulse told her otherwise—she was hoping she was mistaken.

But the man who jumped off the horse had such grace and innate athleticism that her mouth dried.

He tied the horse to the buggy and then stalked towards her, growing bigger and taller as he did so. Right up until the moment that he ripped aside the material covering his mouth and face Sylvie was still hoping it was anyone but...*him*. Of course he'd found her. This man seemed to have a heat-seeking radar, able to pin her to the spot no matter where she was.

'You damned little fool. What the *hell* did you hope to achieve by this stunt?'

She tried to ignore how Arkim's almost savage appearance made her feel as if she was losing it completely. He looked even more ridiculously handsome against this unforgiving backdrop.

She shouted back. 'I was trying to get away from *you*, in case it wasn't completely obvious.'

Arkim's eyes glittered like obsidian. 'In a golf buggy? With none of your things?' He was scathing. 'Did you really think you could just bounce merrily across hundreds of miles of desert and roll into the nearest petrol station to refuel?'

Humiliated beyond measure, Sylvie launched herself at Arkim, hands balled into fists and beating against his chest.

He caught her arms easily and held her immobile. Tension crackled between them, and for a heart-stopping moment Sylvie thought he was going to kiss her—but then a piercing sound shattered the air and they both looked up to see two Jeeps coming towards them over the top of the dune, horns blasting.

Sylvie felt so jittery all she wanted was to escape back to the castle as quickly as possible and lock herself in her rooms. She was caught between a rock and a hard place. Literally. The thought didn't amuse her.

The Jeeps pulled up and concerned-looking staff spilled out. Sylvie immediately felt guilty for having precipitated this search.

Arkim wordlessly led her over to the nearest vehicle and said a few words to the driver. Then he opened up the back door for her. When she would have expected to get in, he handed her a bottle of water. She looked at him and he was grim.

'Drink, you'll be dehydrated.'

Sylvie couldn't argue with that, and she was thirsty, so she took several large gulps. Then Arkim reached into the back of the Jeep again and pulled out a long white robe. He thrust it at her.

'I'm supposed to put this on?' Sylvie said waspishly.

Arkim's expression darkened. 'Yes. You're already burning.'

Her skin *was* still prickling, but Sylvie was afraid that it was more to do with his effect on her than the sun—even though when she looked her arms were ominously pink.

Mutinously she pulled on the long-sleeved robe, and was surprised at how much cooler she felt instantly—which was crazy when she was pulling on *more* clothes.

Then he was unwinding his *keffiyeh* from his head, and before she could stop him he'd placed it over her hair, like a shawl. He started to wind it around her head, tucking it in, until there was only one long piece left that he drew across her mouth and tucked in at the back.

She was effectively swaddled. And it was only then that she realised that the Jeeps were driving off into the distance, towing the buggy behind them. Arkim's scent was disturbing, and all around her. The thought that this fabric had been across his mouth was almost too intimate to take in.

He held his horse by the reins and was leading it over. Sylvie pulled down the material covering her mouth. 'What are you doing? Where are the Jeeps going?'

He stopped in front of her, the huge horse prancing behind him. 'We are going for a little trip.'

Before she could ask more, Arkim had his hands around her waist and was lifting her effortlessly onto the horse. His sheer strength took her breath away and she clung to the saddle, her brain reeling at being so high up. She hadn't been on a horse since she was a teenager...

Arkim put his foot in the stirrup and vaulted on behind her, his agility awesome. And suddenly he was all around her. Strong muscled thighs gripping hers, his torso against her back, his arms coming around her to take the reins.

'Cover your mouth.'

Sylvie was too stunned to move. 'Wh—where are we going?'

Arkim angled himself so he could see her and made a rude sound. 'Don't you *ever* do anything you're told?' The material was firmly pulled back over her mouth and he said, 'It'll stop sand getting in.'

Sylvie couldn't say anything else, because Arkim was turning the horse around and they were galloping in the opposite direction from where the Jeeps had gone. For a semi-hysterical moment Sylvie thought that perhaps she'd pushed Arkim so far he was just going to dump her in the desert and leave her to die a slow, painful death.

Gradually, though, as they galloped into the seeming nothingness of the sandy landscape, almost against her will she felt herself relaxing into Arkim's body, letting him take her weight. One of his arms was around her torso, holding her to him, and she felt the intimate space between her legs soften and moisten.

She was fast losing all sense of reality. The real world and civilisation felt very far away.

After about twenty minutes Arkim drew the stallion to a stop, its muscles quivering under Sylvie's legs. He got off the horse and Sylvie looked down to see his arms outstretched towards her. His mouth was stern.

'Bring your leg over the horse, Sylvie.'

She wanted to disobey, but she knew Arkim would pull her off the horse anyway. Better to do it with a modicum of decorum and not let him see how intimidated she was. And she was scared... Even though she knew—in some way she didn't like to investigate—that he wouldn't harm her.

Her hands landed on Arkim's wide shoulders and his hands clamped around her waist as he lifted her down as effortlessly as before. She saw the reins on the ground and said nervously, 'Won't the horse just go?'

'Aziz won't move unless I say so. And we won't be long.' Arkim's tone brooked no disobedience—from her or the horse.

Sylvie broke away from Arkim's hands. The *keffiyah* was still around her mouth and she pulled it down as she looked around at a sea of nothing but blue sky and dunes.

'Why are we here?'

Arkim planted himself in front of her, hands on hips. 'Because this is where you would have ended up if the buggy hadn't run out of fuel. This is where we might have found you in two days, if we were lucky enough, dehydrated and burnt to a crisp.'

Sylvie looked at him and shivered. 'You're exaggerating.'

Arkim looked livid. He grabbed her arms with his hands. 'No, I'm not. Men who know this area, who have lived here for years, can still get caught out by the desert. Right now it looks calm, wouldn't you agree?'

Sylvie nodded hesitantly.

Arkim's mouth thinned. 'It's anything but. There's a sandstorm due to hit any day now. Have you ever been in a sandstorm?'

She shook her head.

'Imagine a tidal wave coming towards you—except in this case it's made of sand and debris, not water. You'd be obliterated in seconds. Suffocated.'

Genuine horror and fear finally made her realise just how reckless she'd been. She seized on the surge of anger. He made her feel as if she was a tiny ship bobbing about in a huge raging sea.

'Okay, fine—I get it. What I did was foolish and reckless and silly. I didn't know. I didn't mean to put everyone to so much trouble...' A very unwelcome sense of vulnerability made her lash out. 'But, in case you don't remember, it's *your* fault I'm even here!'

Arkim looked down at that beautiful but defiant face and felt such a mix of things that he was dizzy. He shook his head, but nothing rational would come to the surface. All he could see was *her*.

He gave in to the urgent dictates of his blood and lowered his mouth to the lush contours of hers—and drowned.

His tongue swept into her mouth in a marauding move and he quickly became oblivious to everything except the rough stroke of his tongue against Sylvie's, demanding a response.

She resisted him for long seconds, but he felt her gradually relax, as if losing a battle with herself. Once again there was an almost unbelievable hesitance—as if she didn't know what to do. The thought that she could do this—get under his skin so easily, make him doubt himself—made Arkim's blood boil.

He held the back of her covered head and put his hand to where her neck met her shoulder in an unashamedly possessive move, his thumb reaching for and finding that hectic pulse-beat, which was telling him that no matter how ingrained it was in her to act, she couldn't control *everything*.

And finally he felt her arms relax and start to climb around his neck, bringing her body into more intimate contact with his. Her mouth softened and she...acquiesced. The triumph was heady. Her tongue stroked his sweetly, sucking him deep—as deep as he imagined the exquisite clasp of her body would be around his in a more intimate caress.

He wanted to throw her down on the ground right here and pull up that robe, yank down her jeans, until he could find his release. The desire was so strong he shook in a bid to rein it in. And that brought him back from the brink of losing it completely.

Reality slammed into him. He was in the middle of the desert, under the merciless sun, about to ravage this woman. Make her his...brand her like some kind of animal.

He wanted to push her away from him and yet never let her go.

He hated her. He wanted her.

He pulled back from the kiss even though everything in his body and his blood protested at the move. He felt the unrelenting beat of the sun on his head. Her eyes opened after a moment, wide and blue...and that intriguing blue-green. Her cheeks were flushed. Lips swollen.

And then suddenly she tensed and scrambled free of his arms. Arkim might almost have laughed—even now she was intent on playing this game of push and pull. Acting her little heart out.

'Have you forgotten that you're a civilised man?'

Even her voice sounded suitably shaky. But Arkim barely cast her a glance as he reached for the horse's reins. 'I don't have to be civilised here.'

That was why he'd brought her here in the first place—because he didn't trust himself around her in more civilised surroundings. It was as if he'd known the desert was the only place big enough to contain what he felt for her.

He picked up the reins, ignoring the dull throb of unsatisfied desire in his system...the way his arousal pressed against his trousers under his robe.

'You really can't turn it off, can you?'

Sylvie scowled at him. She should have looked ridiculous. The *keffiyah* was askew on her head, and slivers of bright red curling tendrils of hair peeped out from under its folds. She crossed her arms. 'Turn what off?'

'Your constant need to act out some role—pretend you don't want this.'

'I'm *not* acting. And I *don't* want this! I don't know what happened there…a moment of sunstroke…but it won't be happening again.'

Arkim almost felt pity for her. He reached out and rubbed a thumb back and forth over her plump lower lip. 'Oh, don't worry—it'll be happening again, and you'll be fully participant in it when it does.'

Sylvie slapped his hand away. She might have screamed at his arrogance, but he was lifting her up onto the horse again before she could take another breath. And, in any case, what could she say after she'd just melted all over him?

It was pathetic. *She* was pathetic. She turned to mush when he came near her. So she'd just have to keep him at a distance.

But then he got up on the horse behind her again, and predictably Sylvie's body went into a paroxysm of anticipation as one arm snaked around her torso, holding her to him, and his other hand expertly gathered the reins to urge the horse on. Of course he would *have* to be an expert horseman too. Was there anything this man *couldn't* do? Apart from act in a civil manner to her?

His lower body was pressed against her backside now, and she could feel the thrust of something unmistakably hard. Her face flamed, and it had nothing to do with the sun. She yanked the material of the *keffiyah* back over her mouth. He wouldn't have to ask her to cover up. She'd never uncover herself again in this man's presence.

CHAPTER FOUR

SYLVIE SAT CURLED up on one of the vast couches in the living area of her suite. When she'd returned to her rooms a couple of hours ago she'd found Halima waiting for her, with ointment for her sun-tender skin and some lunch snacks—and plenty of water. Arkim's efficiency at work. Afterwards she'd changed into loose pants and layered on a couple of her sleeveless workout tops to keep her arms bare.

On their return Arkim had taken her into an expansive stables area at the back of the castle, and when he'd helped Sylvie off the horse she'd felt wobbly-legged and suitably chastened after being shown the very real dangers of the desert.

Arkim hadn't accompanied her back to the castle; he'd sent for one of his staff to do it. Sylvie had recognised him as one of the drivers of the Jeeps and had apologised to him for having dragged them out to look for her. She wasn't even sure if he'd understood her, but he'd shaken his head and looked embarrassed, as if it was nothing.

The night was falling outside now: the sky was a stunning deep violet colour and stars were appearing. Questions abounded in her head. Questions about Arkim. Seeing him against this backdrop was more intriguing than she liked to admit. And she hated to acknowledge it but she was also fascinated by the barely repressed emotions below the surface of his urbanity. He was different here. More raw. It should be intimidating. But it excited her.

What was his connection to this place? And if he had a connection here, how could he—a man who had this desert in his blood, so timeless and somehow base—agree to marry purely for business and strategic reasons?

A noise made her tense and she looked round to see the object of her thoughts in the doorway to her living room. Dressed in a robe again, with his head bare, he looked...powerful. Mysterious.

Sylvie's belly tightened. 'Come to check your prisoner is still here?'

Arkim's mouth lifted slightly at one corner, as if he were wryly amused, and Sylvie felt it like a punch to the gut.

'Somehow I don't think even *you* would be so foolish as to try and escape again.'

Sylvie scowled. 'Next time I'll prepare better.'

His smile faded. 'There won't be a next time—believe me. You won't be leaving until I do.'

She stood up, frustration running through her blood. 'Look, this is crazy. I need to get back to Paris. I have to—'

Arkim interrupted her. 'You have to eat.'

She could see staff now, coming up behind him, carrying things.

He stood aside and said, 'I've arranged for dinner to come to you this evening. We'll have it on the terrace.'

She felt completely impotent. What could she do? Storm off to another part of the castle in protest?

She preceded Arkim out to where the staff were setting up on the terrace, and when she saw lanterns being lit, sending out soft golden light, her heart flipped. She'd imagined this seductive scenario...

Plates of fragrant steaming food were being placed on a low table and the scents teased Sylvie's nostrils. She was an unashamed foodie, and the prospect of an exotic feast was too much temptation to resist.

Halima arrived then, with a bottle of champagne which she put in an ice bucket by the table. Sylvie scowled at it, just as Arkim came into her line of vision and held out a hand.

'Please, take a seat.'

Sylvie sat down cross-legged on a low chair, and watched as Arkim lowered himself athletically into a similar pose on the other side of the delicately carved table. It should have made him look less manly, but of course it didn't.

'How are your arms?'

She glanced down, noting with relief that the vivid pink had faded and they weren't so hot. In this day and age of knowledge of sun damage she'd been very stupid.

She said, 'Much better. Halima's ointment was very effective.'

She looked at Arkim and words of apology for running off earlier trembled on her tongue. But he wasn't looking at her—he was piling a plate high with different foods before handing it to her. Like a coward, she swallowed the words back and took the plate, telling herself that he would only spurn an apology.

There was a faint popping sound as he expertly opened the champagne and poured her a glass of the sparkling wine. She accepted it after a moment's hesitation.

Arkim arched a brow. 'You don't like champagne?'

'I don't drink much of any alcohol, I never really acquired the taste.'

Arkim made a noise and she looked at him, seeing him fill his own glass as he said, 'You forget that I've seen you inebriated.'

Sylvie frowned, and then that night in the garden flooded back. Hotly she defended herself. 'My shoe got stuck in the ground. I was still on antibiotics from a chest infection that night—the last thing I'd have done was drink alcohol.'

He just looked at her, eyes narrowed, and she glared at him. After a long moment he shrugged and said, 'It hardly matters now, in any case.'

Sylvie was disconcerted by how much it *did* matter to her. She looked away from him and put down her glass without taking a sip, choosing to focus on the food instead and trying to block him out. *Ha!* As if *that* was possible.

Arkim could see how tense Sylvie's body was as she resolutely avoided his eye and picked at the food. Her jaw was so tight he thought she might break it if she had to chew. Her vibrant hair was piled high in a haphazard bun, tendrils trailing down to frame her face. His fingers itched to undo the knot and let her hair fall around her shoulders and down her back.

He diverted his attention from the urge he felt to undo that knot and watched with growing incredulity, and something much earthier, as Sylvie seemed to be absorbed by the food—spearing large morsels and evidently taking extreme pleasure out of the discovery of the various tastes. It was incredibly sensual to watch.

She seemed to be completely oblivious to Arkim and he sat back slightly, the better to observe her. He knew she *wasn't* oblivious to him, though— it was there in the tension of her body, and in the pulse beating under the delicate pale skin of her throat.

He'd noticed for the first time this evening that his impression of her being tall actually wasn't correct. He might have registered it before if she hadn't distracted him so easily, but she'd always seemed a lot taller. Maybe it was because she consistently stood up to him in a way no one else did.

That revelation wasn't welcome. It made him think of the fact that he'd overheard her trying to apologise to a member of his staff earlier. He'd have assumed it was for show, but she had been almost out of his earshot, so patently not doing it for his benefit.

Sylvie was actually only just above average height, and her whole frame was on the petite side. He didn't like the way this fact made his conscience smart a little. It made him see a vulnerability he'd blocked out before, and reminded him of the way her stepmother had slapped her in the church...

She leaned forward at that moment, to get some bread, and her full breasts swayed with the movement. Arkim's whole body seemed to sizzle, and he was reminded of exactly who he was dealing with here—a mistress of selfishness and manipulation.

'You like the food?' he asked now, in some kind of effort to wrench his mind off Sylvie's physical temptations, angry with himself.

She glanced at him—a flash of blue and green. She nodded and swallowed what she was eating. Her voice was low, husky, when she said, 'It's delicious. I've never tasted flavours like this before.'

'The lamb is particularly good.'

He speared a morsel of succulent meat with his

fork and held it across the table. When she reached for it with her hand he pulled it back and looked at her. She scowled.

'Coward,' Arkim said softly.

Something in him exulted when he saw the fire flash in her eyes as she took the bait and leant across the table to take the piece of meat off his fork and into her mouth.

Her loose tops swayed, giving Arkim an unrestricted view of her lace-clad breasts. Full and perfectly shaped. She moved back before he could make a complete fool of himself by grabbing her and hauling her across the table.

Her cheeks were flaming. And he didn't think it was from the spices in the lamb. Their mutual chemistry was obvious. So why would she fight it like this?

He leant back on one arm again. She took a sip of champagne and he watched the long, graceful column of her throat work, jealous of even that small movement. She might have passed for eighteen, with her face free of make-up.

Something niggled at him—where was the *femme fatale*? So far he had to admit that the Sylvie he had here was nothing like the woman who had provoked him beyond measure each time he'd seen her before. Not least when she'd appeared in the church, dressed from head to toe in motorcycle gear. The soft black leather jacket and trousers had moulded to her body in a way that had been indecent—and even more so in a church.

He'd expected her to be a lot more sophisticated, knowing... Giving in to her situation and manipulating him as much as she could. That was how the women he knew operated—ultimately they would follow the path of least resistance and take as much as they could.

That was what had attracted him to Sophie Lewis and made him believe he could marry her—her complete lack of guile or artifice. A rare thing in this world.

And that was as far as the attraction had gone.

Arkim ignored the voice. But he had to acknowledge uncomfortably that if the wedding had gone ahead and he'd married Sophie Lewis he wouldn't be here now with her sister. And for a sobering and very unpalatable moment Arkim couldn't regret that fact.

A deeper, darker truth nudged at his consciousness—the very real doubts he'd had himself about the wedding as it had come closer and closer. But he wasn't a man who spent fruitless time wondering about what might have been. And he didn't entertain doubts. He made decisions and he dealt in reality, and this was now his reality.

Sylvie was avoiding looking at him and he hated that.

He said, 'Your eyes...I've never seen that before.'

Sylvie was straining with every muscle she had not to let Arkim see how much he was getting to her, lounging on the other side of the table as he was, like some kind of robed demigod. When she'd leant across the table—provoked into taking that food off his fork—and she'd seen him looking down her top, she'd almost combusted.

Distracted, and very irritated, she said, 'They're just eyes, Arkim. Everyone has them. Even you.'

She risked a look and saw that half-smile again. *Lord*.

'Yes, but none as unusual as you. Blue and blue-green.'

Sylvie hated the frisson she felt to think of him studying her eyes. 'My mother had it too. It's a condition called heterochromia iridum. There's really nothing that mysterious about it.'

Arkim frowned now. 'Your mother was French, wasn't she?'

Sylvie nodded, getting tenser now, thinking of Arkim's judgmental gaze turning on her deceased mother. Sophie must have mentioned it to him.

'Yes, from just outside Paris.'

'And how did your parents meet?'

Sylvie glared at him. 'You're telling me you don't know?'

He shrugged lightly and asked, 'Should I?'

For a moment she processed that nugget. Maybe he genuinely didn't.

From what she'd learnt of this man, he would not hesitate to take advantage of another excuse to bash her—so, anticipating his scathing reaction, she lifted her chin and said, 'She was a dancer— for a revue in Paris that was in the same building where I now dance. It had a different name when she was there and the show was...of its time.'

'What does that mean?' he drawled derisively. 'Not so much skin?'

Sylvie cursed herself for being honest. Why couldn't she just have said her mother had been a nurse, or a secretary? Because, her conscience answered her, her mother would never have hidden her true self. And neither would Sylvie.

'Something like that. It was more in the line of vintage burlesque.'

'And how did your father meet her? He doesn't strike me as the kind of man who frequents such establishments.'

Sylvie pushed down the hurt as she recalled sparkling memories full of joy—her father laughing and swinging her mother around in their back garden. She smiled sweetly and said, 'Just goes to show that you can't always judge a book by its cover.'

Arkim had the grace to tilt his glass towards her slightly and say, 'Touché.'

She played with her champagne glass, which was still half full. She grudgingly explained, 'He was in Paris on a business trip and went with some of his clients to the show. He saw my mother... asked her out afterwards...that was it.'

Sylvie would never reveal the true romance of her parents' love story to this cynical man, but the fact was that her father had fallen for Cécile Devereux at first sight—a *coup de foudre*—and had wooed her for over a month before her mother had finally deigned to go out with him—an English businessman a million miles removed from the glamorous Cécile Devereux's life. Yet she'd fallen in love with him too. And they'd been happy. Ecstatically.

Familiar emotion and vulnerability rose up inside Sylvie now and she knew she didn't want Arkim to probe any further into her precious memories.

She took a sip of champagne and looked at him. 'What about *your* parents?'

Arkim's expression immediately darkened. It was visible even in the flickering light of the dozens of candles and lanterns.

'As you've pointed out—you know very well who my father is.'

Sylvie flushed when she recalled throwing that in Arkim's face in her father's study. She refused to cower, though. This man had judged her from the moment he'd laid eyes on her.

She thought of how he was doing everything he could to distance himself from his parent and she was doing everything to follow in her mother's footsteps. The opposite sides of one coin.

'I don't know about your mother—were they married?'

His look could have sliced through steel. Clearly this wasn't a subject he relished, and it buoyed her up to see him lose that icy control he seemed to wield so effortlessly. It reminded her of how she'd wanted to shatter it when she'd first met him. Well, it had shattered all right—taking her with it.

Arkim's tone was harsh. 'She died in childbirth, and, no, they weren't married. My father doesn't *do* marriage. He's too eager to hang on to his fortune and keep his bedroom door revolving.'

Sylvie didn't like the little dart of sympathy she felt to hear that his mother had died before he'd even known her. She moved away from that kernel of information. 'So, you grew up in America?'

His mouth tightened. 'Yes. And in England, in a series of boarding schools. During holidays in LA I was a captive audience for my father's debauched lifestyle.'

Sylvie winced inwardly. There was another link in the chain to understanding this man's prejudices.

Hesitantly she said, 'You've never been close, then?'

Arkim's voice could have chilled ice. 'I haven't seen him since I was a teenager.'

Sylvie sucked in a breath.

Before she could think how to respond, Arkim inserted mockingly, 'Living with him taught me a valuable lesson from an early age: that life isn't some fairytale.'

The extent of his cynicism mocked Sylvie's tender memories of her own parents. 'Most people don't experience what you did.'

His eyes glittered like black jewels. He looked completely relaxed, but she could sense the tension in his form.

The question was burning her up inside. 'Is that one of the reasons why you agreed to marry Sophie? Because you don't believe real marriages can exist?'

'Do you?' he parried.

Sylvie cursed her big mouth and glanced away. She longed to match his cynicism with her own, but the truth was that even after witnessing how grief had torn her father apart she *had* seen real love for a while.

She looked back. 'I think sometimes, yes, they can. But even a happy marriage can be broken apart very easily.' *By devastating illness and death.*

He looked at her consideringly for a long moment and she steeled herself. But then he asked, 'What was your mother like?'

Sylvie's insides clenched harder. She looked at her glass.

'She was amazing. Beautiful, sweet...kind.' When Arkim didn't respond with some cutting comment, she went on, 'I always remember her perfume...it was so distinctive. My father used to buy it in the same shop for her whenever he was in Paris. It was opposite the Ritz hotel, run by a beautiful Indian woman. He took me with him once. I remember she had a small daughter...' Her mouth quirked as she got lost in the memory. 'I used to sit at my mother's feet and watch her get ready to go out with my father. She used to hum all the time. French songs. And she would dance with me...'

'Sounds just like one of those fairytales—too good to be true.'

Arkim's voice broke through the memories like a rude klaxon. Sylvie's head jerked up. She'd forgotten where she was for a moment, and with whom.

'It *was* true. And good.'

She hated it that her voice trembled slightly. She wouldn't be able to bear it now if Arkim was to delve further and ask about her mother's death. That excruciating last year, when cancer had turned her mother into a shadow of her former self, would haunt Sylvie for the rest of her life. She'd lost both her parents from that moment.

She felt prickly enough to attack. 'Why did you agree to marry my sister? Really?'

Arkim was expressionless. 'For all the reasons I have already explained to you.'

Beyond irritated, and frustrated at the way he made her feel, Sylvie put down her napkin and stood up, walking over to the wall. She heard him move and turned around to face him, feeling jittery.

He stood a few feet away. Too close for comfort. Before she could say anything, Arkim folded his arms and said, 'I won't deny I had my doubts...'

Sylvie went still.

'That night in the study, when you found me... I wasn't altogether certain that I was going to go through with it. But then you appeared...' Something like anger flashed in his eyes. 'Let's just say that you helped me make up my mind.'

Sylvie reeled. He might have called it off? And then his words registered. Anger flared. 'So it was *my* fault?'

He ignored that. 'Why did you break up the wedding? Was it purely for spite?'

The realisation that Arkim might have called the whole thing off was mixing with her anger, diluting it. Making her heart beat faster. Words trembled on her lips. Words that would exonerate her. But she couldn't do it; she'd promised her sister.

She lifted her chin. 'All you need to know is that if I had to do it over again I wouldn't hesitate.'

Arkim's face hardened even more. He didn't like that. But his drawling voice belied his expression. 'The motorbike was a cute touch. Did you learn how to ride one especially for dramatic effect?'

Sylvie flushed. 'I used to have one in Paris—to get around. Until it got stolen. I hired one that day…more for expediency than anything else.'

He sneered now. 'You mean a quick, cowardly getaway so you didn't have to deal with the fall-out…?'

Before Sylvie could formulate a response, Halima and some other discreet staff appeared at that moment, defusing the tension a little, and removed the remains of their dinner from the table.

When they were gone Sylvie was still facing Arkim, like an adversary in a boxing ring. The revelation that she'd inadvertently influenced his decision to marry Sophie was crowding everything else out of her head. Presumably it had been because she'd reminded him of exactly the kind of woman he *didn't* want. And that stung.

She pushed down her roiling emotions and tried to appeal to his civilised side. 'Arkim...you've made your point. You need to let me go now.'

His expression remained as hard as granite. Unforgiving. Sylvie shivered. This man wasn't civilised here.

And then he said, 'I've paid a substantial sum of money for your presence and I believe that I'd like to see you dance for me.' The shape of his mouth turned bitter. 'After all, thousands have seen you dance, so why shouldn't I?'

The thought of performing in front of this man made Sylvie go cold, and then hot. 'Now?' Her voice squeaked slightly.

A ghost of a smile touched his lips. 'No, tomorrow evening. You'll perform a very *private* dance. Just for me.'

She straightened her spine. 'If you're expecting a lap dance, I hate to disappoint you but I really don't do that kind of thing.'

He moved close enough to reach out and trail a finger down over her cheek and jaw, and said softly, 'I'm looking forward to seeing what you *do* do.'

She slapped his hand down, terrified of the way his touch made her melt so easily. Terrified he'd kiss her again. 'And why on earth should I do anything you ask me to?'

Arkim's jaw clenched, and then he said baldly, 'Because you owe me, and I'm collecting.'

The following evening Halima held up one of Sylvie's rhinestone-encrusted outfits and stroked it reverently. 'This is so beautiful.'

The thought of the robed young woman wearing it, baring her skin so comprehensively, made Sylvie feel a little uncomfortable, and she gently took the garment out of Halima's hands to hang it up, along with the other costumes the girl had insisted on taking out of her suitcase.

She hadn't been able to eat since breakfast that morning, and her belly had been doing somersaults all day at the thought of dancing for Arkim. She'd realised that of course he'd be expecting her to rebel, refuse. And then maybe he'd initiate another cosy dinner and tell her more things about himself that would put her on uneven ground where her feelings towards him were concerned.

As she'd lain in bed last night and gone over everything he'd told her she had found her antipathy hard to cling on to. So she'd decided to keep him at arm's length and do the opposite of what he was expecting and dance for him. She realised with some level of dark irony that if he was reverse psychoanalysing her, then it was working.

And if Sylvie was being completely honest with herself, a part of her still wanted to provoke Arkim—make him admit that he was just like everyone else.

It was that damned icy façade of his that had sneaked under her skin and made her want to break it apart as soon as he'd looked at her for the first time with such disdain. And where had breaking that control apart got her? To one of the hottest places on earth. About to strip herself bare in front of a man who wanted her, yet despised her.

Words trembled on Sylvie's tongue. Words to instruct Halima to go and tell the Sheikh that she wasn't available this evening after all. But she couldn't back down now.

She surveyed herself in the mirror as Halima clipped a veil behind her head, obscuring her mouth, so only her heavily kohled eyes were visible. Her hair was tucked and hidden under another veil.

Sylvie wondered if Arkim would appreciate the fact that the act she'd decided to do was based on the story of *Scheherazade*. Somehow, she didn't think he'd be amused.

She took a deep breath and turned to Halima. 'Now all I need is a sword...do you think you can find one here?'

The young girl thought for a moment, then brightened. 'Yes!'

Anticipation lay heavy and thick in Arkim's bloodstream as he waited for Sylvie to appear. He'd given instructions for her to be brought to one of the ceremonial rooms, where traditionally the Sheikh would greet and entertain his important guests. The room was open to the elements behind Arkim. Lanterns lit the space with golden flickering shadows.

Just then he noticed that a strong gust of wind whipping through the open space had almost put out one of the candles. The storm. It was coming. It made Arkim feel reckless. Wild. He'd gone out on Aziz earlier that day, tracking it, seeing the wind pick up. The stallion had moved skittishly, wanting to get back to cover.

There was a raised marble dais in the centre

of the room, where the Sheikh would usually sit to greet his guests, and it was also sometimes used for ceremonial performances and dances. Arkim didn't doubt that he was about to bring this space into serious disrepute by having Sylvie dance here, but he couldn't seem to care too much.

He took a sip of his wine. *Where was she?* He tensed at the thought that she was defying him again.

Just as he was about to put down his glass and stand up and go to her, his blood fizzing, she appeared. She was slight and lissom...in bare feet. Arkim blinked as blood roared up into his head and south to another part of his anatomy.

She didn't look in his direction or acknowledge him as she stepped up onto the dais. He wasn't sure what he'd been expecting, but it wasn't this. She was wearing gold figure-hugging trousers that were flared at the ends and partially slit up the sides, embellished with jewels and lace. They sat low on her hips, along with a belt from which tassels dropped and moved and swayed with her body.

Her middle was toned and bare, and encircled with a delicate gold chain that sat just above the curve of her hips. A cropped black top with long trailing sleeves was tied in the front, between her breasts, worn over a gold-coloured and very ornate-looking bra.

Her breasts were...perfection. Full and luscious, beautifully shaped. Her provocative cleavage was framed by the top.

She still hadn't even so much as flicked a glance in his direction, and he noticed properly for the first time that the lower half of her face was obscured by a black veil, and that a black covering also hid her hair. Arkim wanted to rip it off and see those red tresses tumbling around her shoulders.

All that was visible of her face were her heavily kohled eyes. She was bending down now, doing something with speakers, and then a slow, sultry and distinctly Arabic beat filled the space.

Arkim's eyes widened when he saw her pick up a large curved sabre—he'd been too distracted to notice it before. He frowned. It looked disturbingly like the one that hung in the exhibition room that housed all his precious antiques and old weapons.

Sylvie faced away from him now, and all he could see was the tempting curve of her buttocks, the tantalising line of her waist and hips, and that gold chain glinting in the flickering glow of the lamps. And then she lifted the sword high in her hands over her head and slowly turned to face him. Those distinctive eyes met his, and she started to move sinuously to the beat of the music.

And Arkim's brain stuttered to a halt.

He was aware of pale skin, dips and hollows, a toned belly. She played with the huge sword as if it was a baton—twirling it in one hand and then in the other. She was on her knees now, one leg raised at a right angle, and arching her body backwards like a bow, with the sword resting on its tip behind her and her free arm stretched out in front of her. The line of her throat was long and graceful, and curiously vulnerable.

The music seemed to be pounding in time with Arkim's blood. And then it changed and became a little faster, with a different beat.

Sylvie straightened up and bent forward with impressive flexibility, bringing the sword back in front of her to place it on the ground and push it away. And then, still bending forward, she lifted the veil and head covering off her head. She undid the tie on her black top and removed that too.

Now her hair tumbled down, free and wild, and the ornately decorated gold bra was revealed. He could see the faint sheen of perspiration on her pale skin and his insides tightened with pure, unadulterated lust. Would her skin be sheened like that when he joined their bodies for the first time?

She came onto her knees, facing Arkim again, and started undulating her body in a series of movements—hips, arms, chest—disconnected but connected. He'd seen belly dancers before, but never like this. Bright red hair trailed over her shoulders and down to her breasts. He wanted to reach out and curl a tendril around his hand, pull her towards him.

She was looking at him now, but blankly. A sizzle of irritation ran through his blood. When women looked at him, they *looked*.

She moved lithely to her feet and brought her whole body into the dance. This should be boring him to tears. But it wasn't. He hated to realise that he was most likely in the kind of thrall that had mesmerised men for hundreds of years when a woman danced like this for him.

And then he realised it was *her*. There was something profoundly captivating about Sylvie and the way she moved. It was knowing, and yet there was something Arkim couldn't put his finger on...something slightly *off*. As if a piece of the jigsaw was missing.

She'd stopped dancing now, her chest moving rapidly with her breath, her hair tangled in waves and falling down her back as she stood with one hand on her hip and the other stretched out towards him, as if she were offering him something.

She hadn't even stripped. But arousal sat heavy in Arkim's body and bloodstream. He felt like a fool. Sylvie had told him that she didn't do lap dances, but somehow that was exactly what he had expected. Something tawdry and fitting for the picture he'd built up of her in his head.

But this whole performance had been sweetly titillating—like a throwback to a more innocent time. A time that Arkim had never had the pleasure of knowing. He'd never really experienced innocence. His own had been corrupted when he had been so young.

Anger rushed through him and he stood up. He did a slow hand-clap and then said, as equably as he could, 'Who exactly are you trying to fool with a routine suited to the top of a table in a restaurant?'

Sylvie's arm dropped and she looked at him, cheeks flushed. Arkim's body throbbed all over. But he held on to what tiny bit of control he had— rigidly.

Her gaze narrowed on him. 'I take it that you didn't care for it, then? Too bad you can't get your money back.'

Her voice was breathy, and there was something defiant in those flashing blue-green eyes. It sent his churning cauldron of emotions into overdrive. She was taunting him. He thought of all the people she'd bared herself to, and yet she wouldn't for him. The thought that she might have an inkling of just how badly he wanted her scored him deep inside.

He didn't want to go near Sylvie for fear of what might happen if he did. As if some beast inside him might be unleashed and she'd see just how close to the edge of his control he was. He felt feral. As if he needed desperately to prove to himself that she was who he believed she was.

'You'll dance again, Sylvie. And this time you'll perform exactly as you do for the thousands of people who have seen *all* of you. I won't accept anything less. Be back here in half an hour.'

CHAPTER FIVE

SYLVIE WATCHED ARKIM stalk out of the huge space, adrenalin still fizzing in her blood. Vulnerability and frustration vied with her anger at his high-handedness. And a need to wipe the disdainful look off his face.

More anger coursed through her when she thought of what Arkim had been expecting and what he clearly still expected: *You'll perform exactly as you do for the thousands of people who have seen all of you.*

She was surprised he hadn't had a pole installed so she could shimmy up and down it. Clearly she'd done such a good job of doing absolutely *nothing* to amend Arkim's bad opinion of her, she'd merely raised his expectations.

It had taken more nerve than she'd thought she possessed to come in here and dance for him. It had taken all her strength to look at him and through him—even though he'd sat there like some kind of lord and master, surveying her as if she was some morsel for his delectation.

But she'd still been acutely aware of that powerful body, its inherent strength barely leashed. He'd dressed in western style, in dark trousers and an open-necked shirt. And somehow, after seeing him in nothing but pristine three-piece suits and then the traditional Arabic tunic, it was a little shocking—as if he was unravelling, somehow.

Suddenly there was a flurry of movement as staff entered the cavernous space and rushed to close the huge open doors.

Sylvie had been so caught up in her own thoughts that she hadn't noticed how the sky had darkened outside—dramatically. There was so much electricity in the air she could swear it was sparking along her skin.

And then Halima appeared, a look of excitement on her pretty face. 'The Sheikh has told me to help you. We must close all your doors and windows—the storm is coming.'

As Halima ushered her out of the room, eager to do her Sheikh's bidding, Sylvie's rage spiked— as if in tandem with the escalating weather outside. If Arkim wanted a damn lap dance so badly, then maybe she should give him exactly what he wanted.

They got back to Sylvie's rooms, and Halima was about to close the French doors but turned around, eyes wide. 'You can see the sandstorm coming!'

'Really?' Curiosity distracted Sylvie momentarily and she went to the doors to look outside. She sucked in a breath when a powerful gust of wind made the curtains flap. She hadn't noticed how strong the winds had become.

'Look—see there? In the distance?'

Sylvie followed Halima's finger and saw what looked like a vast cloud against the darkening sky. It took her eyes several seconds to adjust to the fact that it was a bank of sand, racing across the desert towards them. It was like a special effect in a movie.

'My God...' she breathed, more in awe than in fear at the sight. 'Will we be okay?'

Halima shut the doors firmly and nodded. 'Of course. This castle has withstood much worse. We will be quite safe inside, and by morning it will be gone. You'll see.'

Sylvie shivered at the thought of all that energy racing across the desert—the fury she'd seen in the cloud-like shape. Not unlike the fury she'd seen in Arkim's eyes...

Halima left Sylvie to get ready, telling her she must make sure all the other doors and windows were closed.

Sylvie was grateful for that when she surveyed her outfit in the mirror a short time later. She might have winced if she hadn't still been so angry.

She'd customised one of her short skirts and now it barely grazed the tops of her thighs. The rest of her legs were covered in over-the-knee black socks. She wore a simple white shirt, knotted just under her bust, leaving her midriff bare. Underneath the skirt she wore a pair of black dance shorts, embellished with costume gems sewn into the edges, and under the shirt she wore a glittering black bra top.

She tied her hair back now, in a high ponytail. Her eyes were still heavily kohled, lashes long and dark. Lips bright red.

She felt like a total fraud, just aping what she'd seen in a million images and movies as to what constituted a lap dance outfit. It was ridiculously similar to something a famous pop-star had worn in one of her videos.

The fact was that the L'Amour revue prided itself on doing avant-garde strip routines, burlesque in nature. They didn't do anything as hokey as this. Sylvie's mouth firmed—Arkim clearly wasn't appreciative of the more subtle side of her profession.

Just then there was a knock at the door and Sylvie grabbed for her robe, slipping it on over her clothes. She didn't want Halima to see her like this. She felt tawdry.

The girl appeared. 'The Sheikh is ready for you, Miss Devereux.'

Sylvie tightened the belt of her robe and took a deep breath. 'Thank you.'

But as she walked to the ceremonial room again, behind the young girl, she felt the anger start to drain away. Doubts crept in. She was *not* what Arkim thought she was, and yet here she was—letting him goad her into pretending to be something she wasn't.

Because he'd never believe you, inserted a small voice.

She was at the door now, and her circling thoughts faded as Halima gently nudged her over the threshold. The door closed behind her. The interior was darker than it had been, with the encroaching storm turning the world black outside. Too late to back out now. Girding her loins, Sylvie straightened her shoulders and walked in.

Arkim was sitting in his chair again, with a table beside him holding more wine and food. The anger surged back. He was so arrogant. Demanding. Judgemental. Cold.

She did her best to avoid his eyes, but she was burningly aware of him. He looked dark and unreadable when she sneaked a glance at his face. He seemed so in control. As if nothing would ruffle his cool.

Sylvie *badly* wanted to ruffle his cool.

She put on her music again, aware of the tension spiking in the room when the slow, sultry, sexy beat filled the space. She saw the chair that she'd asked Halima to provide in the centre of the dais, and she slowly unbelted her robe and then slid it off, throwing it to one side.

Did she hear an intake of breath coming from his direction?

She ignored it and walked up to the chair, turning to face Arkim with her hands on the back of it. And now she looked him straight in the eye. Unashamed. Exuding confidence even if she was quivering on the inside.

She started to move, using a mixture of what she'd seen some of the other girls do for their routines and her own modern dance moves. And a hefty dose of inspiration from one of her favourite movies of all time: *Cabaret.*

She kept eye contact with Arkim, even though her confidence threatened to dissolve when his gaze moved down, over her body, over her splayed legs as she sat in the chair. She dipped her head down between her legs before coming back up, deliberately making sure her cleavage would be visible, and running her hands up her bare thighs.

His gaze was so black it seemed to suck all the light out of the room—or was that the storm? Sylvie didn't know. She only knew that as his eyes tracked her movements she became more and more emboldened. She felt as if she was becoming one with the music. The throbbing bass beat was deep in her blood…telling her where to move next. Telling her to stand up, to put her hands on the seat of the chair and bend over, while sending a sideways look to Arkim. Telling her to straighten and then arch her back as she pulled her hair tie off so her hair tumbled down around her shoulders.

And telling her to open the buttons on her shirt, down to where it was tied under her breasts, so that they would be revealed.

Something dangerous was pounding through her blood—the same something that had coursed through it that night in the garden, when Arkim had pressed against her, letting her feel how aroused he was by her...even though he disapproved of her.

Sylvie felt powerful—because she could sense his control cracking. Arkim's cheeks were flushed, eyes glittering darkly. Jaw clenched. This was what she wanted...to make him admit he was a hypocrite.

Without really thinking about what she was doing, Sylvie stepped down from the dais and walked over to Arkim. His chin tipped up and their gazes clashed—just as the music faded away and stopped, bursting the bubble of illusion around them.

She knew instantly that she'd made a tactical error. Desperate to try and regain her sense of power, she started to walk away from his chair—but a big hand shot out and gripped her wrist, stopping her in her tracks.

She looked down at him, heart bumping violently. That obsidian gaze glittered up at her, and she saw the fire in their depths. The knowledge that she'd managed to ruffle him wasn't as satisfying as she'd expected when she was this close to him.

He stood up and they were almost touching. The air sizzled.

'What the *hell*,' he said in a low voice, 'do you think you're doing?'

The disgust Sylvie read in his eyes made her pull her wrist free of his grip with a jerk. She was aware that the huge sand cloud was approaching closer and closer through the massive windows behind Arkim, about to envelop them totally, blotting everything out. It made her feel reckless—as if everything was about to be altered for ever.

'Isn't this what you expected of me?' she asked tauntingly. 'I'm giving you exactly what you want.'

'*Exactly* what I want?' he asked.

And before she could say anything, just before the sandstorm inexorably claimed the castle in its path, Arkim speared both hands into her hair, angling her face up to his.

'I'll show you exactly what I want,' he said gutturally.

* * *

Arkim crushed Sylvie's mouth under his, his need too great to be gentle or finessed. He wanted to devour her.

Her lips were soft, but she kept her mouth closed and there was tension in her body. Damn her. She would *not* deny him. Not after that cheap little show. Yet even in spite of the tackiness he'd still been turned on. *Again.* And she was right—he'd asked for this.

That knowledge wasn't welcome.

Neither was her resistance.

Arkim was aware of the changing quality of sound around them. How everything was muffled. The sandstorm must have enveloped them by now. But all of that was secondary to the woman in his arms. The woman who would pay for turning his life upside down.

He took his mouth off hers and looked down to see those extraordinary eyes glaring at him. If he wasn't acutely aware of how her body quivered against his he would have let her go, been done with her. A reluctant lover was not something he was interested in—not that he had much experience of that.

But Sylvie wanted him. It had sparked between

them from the moment their eyes had met—from the moment he'd rejected her outright. And in spite of that rejection they were here now, as if this course had always been inevitable.

There was no turning back until this was done and she'd paid. And he was sated.

He relaxed his hands in her hair, started to subtly massage her skull. It felt fragile under his hands.

'What are you doing?' she said huskily.

Her hands were against his chest, but she wasn't pushing him away. His arousal was so hard he ached with the need to sheathe himself inside her body, feel her contract around him. But her innate fragility did something to him…it tempered his anger, turned it into a need to seduce. To make her acquiescent.

'I'm making love to you.'

Her hands pushed against his chest now. 'Well, I don't want to be made love to.'

Arkim shook his head, his fingers all the while massaging her skull in slow, methodical movements. 'You've admitted you want me. And I think you *do* want to be made love to—very much. After all, you're a highly sexed woman… aren't you, Sylvie?'

Sylvie looked up into his eyes. Even in heels

she felt tiny next to him. Puny. Weak. His fingers were in her hair, massaging her... She felt like purring. Not like pushing him away. But she had to. *Highly sexed?* If he found out what she really was—

She went cold at the thought and pushed him again, but his chest was like a steel wall. Immovable. At the same time she was aware that she wasn't scared; the fight to get away from him was as much a fight with herself as it was with him. More so. And he knew it—the bastard.

His hands were moving now...down to her jaw, cradling her face. Something dangerous lurched inside Sylvie—some emotion that had no place there. It seemed to be the hardest thing in the world to free herself completely and move away.

Arkim's scent was heady, masculine. It enticed her on a very basic female level. He didn't even say anything this time. He just bent his head and kissed her again, those sensual lips moving over hers with masterful precision and an expertise she couldn't resist even though she tried.

She tried to keep her mouth closed, like before. But Arkim was biting gently on her lower lip, making it tingle, making her want more... She felt some of her resistance give way, treacherously, and he took advantage like the expert he was—slipping his tongue between her lips, finding hers and setting her world on fire.

His hands moved over her shoulders, down her back, urging her into him, against the hard contours of his body. Her scanty costume offered little protection. She was helplessly responding to his kiss, to the tantalising slide of his tongue against hers, urging her to mimic him, initiate her own contact.

Sylvie couldn't think. Everything was blurry, fuzzy. Except for this decadent pleasure, seeping into her veins and making her feel languorous. Treacherously, she didn't want this moment to stop. *Ever.*

Her hands were moving, lifting of their own volition, sliding around Arkim's neck so that she could press closer. She was aware of her breasts, crushed to his chest, tightening into hard points. One of his hands was on her lower back and it dipped down further, cupping one buttock, squeezing gently. Between her legs she felt hot, moist...

But as Arkim's hand slipped even lower, precariously close to where Sylvie suddenly wanted to feel him explore her, she had a startling moment of clarity—this man hated her. He believed that she was little more than a common tart, debauched and irredeemable, and she was about to let him be more intimate with her than anyone else had ever been.

Disgusted with her lack of control, Sylvie took Arkim by surprise and pushed herself free of his embrace. For a second when he opened his eyes they looked glazed, unfocused, and then they cleared and narrowed on her. She felt hot and dishevelled. And exposed.

She put her arms around herself. 'I told you. I don't want this.'

Colour slashed Arkim's cheekbones. He was grim. 'You want this, all right—you're just determined to send me crazy for wanting it too.'

Something enigmatic lit his eyes, and for a split-second Sylvie had the uncanny impression that it was vulnerability.

That impression was well and truly quashed when he said coldly, 'I don't play games. Go to bed, Sylvie.'

He turned on his heel, and he was walking away when something rogue goaded her to call after him, 'You don't know a thing about me. You think you do, but you don't.'

Arkim stopped and turned around, his face etched in stern lines. It made Sylvie want to run her fingers over them, see them soften. She cursed herself.

'What don't I know?' he asked, with a faint sneer in his tone.

'Things like the fact that I'd never sleep with someone who hates me as much as you do.'

He walked back towards her slowly and Sylvie regretted saying anything. He stopped a few feet away.

'I thought I hated you…especially after what you did to ruin the wedding…but actually I don't feel anything for you except physical desire.'

Sylvie was surprised how strong the dart of hurt was, but she covered it by saying flippantly, 'Oh, wow—thanks for the clarification. That makes it all *so* much better.'

To her surprise, Arkim just looked at her for a long moment, and then he reached for the robe that lay on the ground near their feet and handed it to her, saying curtly, 'Put it on.'

Now he wanted her to cover up… Why didn't that make her feel vindicated in some way?

She slipped her arms into the sleeves and belted the thick material tightly around her waist. Arkim was still looking at her intently, but it had a different quality to any expression she'd seen before. She felt exposed, and a little disorientated. For a moment when he'd handed her the robe she could have sworn he'd seemed almost...apologetic.

As much as she didn't want to hear his scathing response again, she was tired of playing a role that wasn't really her. 'There's something else you don't know.'

Arkim arched a brow.

She took a deep breath. 'I've never actually... stripped. The main act I do in the show is the one with the sword. I do other routines too, but I've never taken all my clothes off. What I did just now...I made it up...I was just proving a point.'

He frowned, shook his head as if trying to clear it. 'Why don't I believe that?'

Sylvie lifted her chin. 'Because you judged me before you even met me, and you have some seriously flawed ideas about what the revue actually is. Why would I lie? It's not as if I have anything to lose where you're concerned.'

She saw a familiar flash of fire come into Arkim's eyes and went on hurriedly.

'The man who runs the revue—Pierre—he knew my mother. They were contemporaries.

When I arrived in Paris I was seventeen years old. He took me under his wing. For the first two years I was only allowed to train with the other dancers. I wasn't allowed to perform. I cleaned and helped keep the books to pay my way.' Sylvie shrugged and looked away, embarrassed that she was telling Arkim so much. 'He's protective of me—like a father figure. I think that's why he doesn't allow me to do the more risqué acts.'

When she glanced back at Arkim his face was inscrutable. Sylvie realised then that he probably resented her telling him anything of the reality of her life.

When he spoke his voice was cool, with no hint of whether or not he believed her. 'Go to bed Sylvie, we're done here.'

She felt his dismissal like a slap in the face and realised with a sense of hollowness that perhaps she should have been honest from the beginning. Then they could have avoided all of this. Because clearly Arkim had no time for a woman who didn't match up to his worst opinions.

He turned to walk away again and she blurted out before she could stop herself, 'What do you mean, "we're done"?'

Arkim stopped and looked at her. He seemed to

be weighing something up in his mind and then he said, 'We'll be leaving as soon as the storm has passed.'

Then he just turned and walked out, leaving Sylvie gaping. *'We'll be leaving...'* She'd done it. She'd provoked him into letting her go. She'd finally made him listen to her—made him listen as she tried to explain who she really was. And now he didn't want to know. Yet instead of relief or triumph all Sylvie felt was...deflated.

'I don't feel anything for you except physical desire.' Arkim's own words mocked him. He couldn't get the flash of hurt he'd seen in Sylvie's eyes out of his head. And he tried. He couldn't deny that it made him feel...guilty. Constricted.

He'd lied. What he felt for her was much more complicated than mere physical desire. It was a tangled mess of emotions, underscored by the most urgent lust he'd ever felt.

He didn't ever say things to hurt women—he stayed well away from any such possibility by making sure that his liaisons were not remotely emotional. Yet he seemed to have no problem lashing out and tearing strips off Sylvie Devereux at every opportunity.

It should be bringing him some sense of pleasure, or satisfaction. But it wasn't. Because he had the skin-prickling feeling that there was something he was missing. Something in Sylvie's responses. He would have expected her to be more petulant. Whiny. More obviously spoilt.

She'd shown defiance, yes, and even though her dash into the desert had been foolhardy she'd shown resilience.

Arkim sat in his book-lined study with its dark, sophisticated furniture and classic original art. He'd always liked this room because it was so far removed from what he remembered of his childhood in LA: his father's vast modern glass mansion in the hills of Hollywood. Everything there was gaudy and ostentatious, the infinity swimming pool full of naked bodies and people high on drugs.

And now he felt like a total hypocrite. Because when Sylvie had stood in front of him in some parody of what strippers wore—because *he'd* all but goaded her into it—he'd been as hard and aching as he could ever remember being. The insidious truth that he really was not so far removed from his father whispered over his skin and made him down a gulp of whisky in a bid to burn it away.

He'd brought her here and asked for it—and she'd called his bluff spectacularly. She was turning him upside down and inside out with her bright blue and green gaze that seemed to sear right through him and tear him apart deep inside. Showing up everything he sought to hide.

The fact that she'd seemed intuitively to sense the maelstrom she inspired within him had galvanised him into kissing her into submission. And yet she'd been the one who had stood there proudly and told him she wouldn't sleep with someone who hated her.

He'd walked away from her just now because she'd shamed him. The irony mocked him.

Arkim couldn't deny it any more: Sylvie made no excuses for what she did and she had more self-worth than most of the people he encountered, who would look down their noses at her. As he had.

When she'd mentioned going to Paris at seventeen he'd felt a tug of empathy and curiosity that no other woman had ever evoked within him. He'd been seventeen when he'd last seen his father. When he'd told him he wasn't coming back to LA and when he'd decided that he would do whatever it took to make it on his own.

Arkim stood up and paced his study. It felt claustrophobic, with the shutters closed against the storm which raged outside—not unlike the turmoil he felt within.

The truth was that he wanted to know more about Sylvie—more about why she did what she did. About her in general. And he'd never felt that same compulsion to know about her sister.

He'd told Sylvie that they'd be leaving as soon as the storm was over—a reflexive reaction to the fact that she affected him in a way he hadn't anticipated. He'd thought it would be easy, that she'd be easy. The truth was that the storm might pass outside, but it would rage inside him until he quenched it.

If he left this place without having her she would haunt him for the rest of his life.

When Sylvie woke the next morning everything was dark and quiet. She got up and padded to the shutters over her windows, not sure what to expect. Maybe the castle would be completely buried in sand? But when she opened them she squinted as beautiful bright blue skies were revealed. What looked like just a thin layer of sand lay over the terrace—the only clue to the formidable weather of the previous evening.

Her mind skittered away from thinking of what else had happened. She wanted to cringe every time she thought of how she must have made such a complete fool of herself—prancing around in those stupid clothes. Even more cringeworthy was recalling how for a few moments she'd got really into it, and had seriously thought she might be turning Arkim on.

But he'd been disgusted. Yet not disgusted enough not to kiss her. And she'd responded— which said dire things about her own sense of self-worth.

Thank God she'd managed to pull back. To show some small measure of dignity. If she hadn't, she could well imagine that Arkim might have laid her down on that stone floor and had her there and then—and discovered for himself just how innocent she was. Sylvie balked at that prospect.

The sunlight streaming into the room reminded her of the fact that Arkim had said they'd be leaving. She sank back on the bed. She'd done it. She'd managed to resist him and disgust him so completely that he was prepared to take her home.

In spite of the mutual physical lust that sparked between them like crackling fire whenever they got close.

She hated to admit it, but that sense of deflation hadn't lifted. Had she enjoyed sparring with Arkim so much? Had she wanted him to take her in spite of what he thought of her? In spite of her brave words last night?

Yes, said a small voice, deep inside. *Because he's connected with you on a level that no other man ever has.*

Sylvie felt disgusted with herself. Was she so wounded inside after her father's rejection of her that this was the only way she could feel desire? For a man who rejected her on every level but the physical?

Someone knocked on the door and she reached for her robe, pulling it on. Halima appeared, smiling, with breakfast on a tray. She set it up on a table near the French doors and opened them wide.

'The storm has passed! It will be good weather for your trip with the Sheikh.'

'My trip...?' Sylvie said quietly, assuming Halima meant her trip home.

The other girl chattered on. 'Yes, the oasis is

so beautiful this time of year…and the way it emerges from the desert—it's like a lush paradise.'

Sylvie frowned, confused. 'Wait—the oasis? Arkim—I mean, the Sheikh isn't leaving to go home today?'

Now Halima looked confused. 'No, he is preparing for his trip and you are going with him. I am to pack enough things for a few days.'

Sylvie's heart-rate picked up pace, along with her pulse. What was Arkim up to now?

She rushed through her breakfast and got washed, and when she re-emerged into the suite Halima was waiting with her bag packed.

Sylvie had dressed in simple cargo pants and a T-shirt. Halima took one look and tutted, saying something about more suitable clothing. Sylvie followed the girl into the dressing room, which Sylvie hadn't explored fully yet, having been intent on using her own clothes. But now Halima was opening the wardrobe doors, and Sylvie gasped when she saw what looked like acres of beautiful fabric: dresses, trousers… All with designer labels.

'Whose are these?' she breathed, letting the silk of one particularly beautiful crimson dress move through her fingers. The thought of them belonging to another woman—or women—was stinging Sylvie in a place that was not welcome.

'They're yours, of course. The Sheikh had them delivered especially for you before your arrival.'

Shock made Sylvie speechless for a moment, and then she said carefully, 'Are you sure they aren't left over from the last woman he had here?'

Halima turned and looked at her, incomprehension clear on her pretty face. 'Another woman? But he's never brought anyone else here.'

Sylvie knew she wasn't lying—she was too sweet...innocent. Her heart started beating even harder. She'd assumed this exotic remote bolthole was one of Arkim's preferred places to decamp with a mistress. She would never have guessed she was the first woman he'd brought here.

'Here—you should change into this.'

Sylvie blinked and saw Halima holding out a long cream tunic with beautiful gold embroidery. Like a more elaborate version of the tunic Arkim had put on her when he'd found her in the desert. *'You're burning.'* His reprimand came back.

'Is this a cultural thing?' Sylvie asked Halima as she slipped out of her trousers.

'Well, yes. Where you're going *is* more rural,

and conservative. But it's also practical. It protects you from the heat and sun.'

'Where you're going.' Sylvie was very aware that she had given no indication to the girl that she was *not* going on this trip. Was she going to just...*go*? Acquiesce? Her pulse tripped again at the thought, and a wave of heat seemed to infuse her skin from toe to head.

The tunic was matched with close-fitting trousers in a beautiful soft cotton material. They too were embroidered with gold. And then Halima was placing a gossamer-light matching shawl around her shoulders. Soft flat shoes completed the outfit.

Sylvie caught sight of herself in a mirror and sucked in a breath. Her hair stood out vibrantly against the light colours of the clothes. She looked...not like herself—but perversely *more* like herself in a way she'd never seen before.

Halima tweaked Sylvie's shawl over her head, and then they were walking down the corridor. She felt a little like a bride being walked to face her fate.

Sylvie chastised herself for being so compliant. Of course she wanted to leave. Of course she had no intention of going off to this admittedly, in-

triguing-sounding oasis with a man who felt nothing for her and yet made her body come alive in
a way that made her want to descend with him
into a pit of fire.

She was going to tell Arkim she had no intention of—

All her thoughts faded to nothing when they
rounded the corner into the main hall and Sylvie
saw Arkim waiting for her.

CHAPTER SIX

HE SIMPLY TOOK her breath away. It was as if she'd never seen him before. He was so tall and exotic, in a long dark blue tunic. Still stern...

It made her yearn for things: to see him smile, unbend. To know more about him. Dangerous things.

The staff left their bags between two Jeeps and melted away into the shadows. Sylvie was aware that this was the moment when she should make it absolutely clear that she had no intention of going with Arkim to this oasis. But she was rooted to the spot—caught and mesmerised by those obsidian eyes.

There was an intense silent conversation happening between them. He was issuing a direct challenge with that fathomless gaze. A challenge that she felt in every pulsing, throbbing beat of her blood. A challenge of the most sensual kind. A challenge to step up and own her femininity in a way she'd never done before. A challenge to go with him.

She felt giddy…breathless. The palms of her hands were damp with perspiration that had nothing to do with the heat.

It came down to this: did she want this man enough to throw her self-respect to the winds and risk the bitter sting of self-recrimination for ever? Did she want to give him the satisfaction of knowing that he was right? That ultimately she couldn't resist him? And did she want to risk the worst kind of rejection?

He moved, and her breath hitched at the sheer grace and beauty of his masculinity. He stopped in front of her. She could see the tension in his form and on his face. It made something inside her soften, uncoil. Closer, like this, he was infinitely more seductive, less formidable. And infinitely harder to resist.

'There are two Jeeps behind me.'

Sylvie had seen them. She nodded.

'The one on the left will take you back to the airfield where we landed the other day—if you want it to. The one on the right is the one I'm taking to the oasis. I told you last night that we'd both be leaving, but I've decided to stay. I want you to stay with me, Sylvie. I think there are things about you that I don't know…that I want to know. And I want *you*. This isn't about the past or the wedding any more. I've made my point. This is about…*us*. And it's been about us since the moment we met.'

His mouth twisted.

'Perhaps our failing all along has been that we didn't pursue this attraction at the time. If we had we wouldn't be standing here now.'

Sylvie's chest contracted with a mixture of volatile emotions. 'Because you'd be married to my sister? That's heinous—'

His finger against her lips stopped her words. He looked disgusted. He took his finger away, but not before Sylvie had the strongest urge to take it into her mouth.

'No. I *never* would have pursued your sister with marriage in mind if we had had an affair.'

Affair. The word hit her hard. Arkim didn't need to clarify the fact that Sylvie would never in a million years be a contender for marriage or a relationship.

Right now she felt very certain that she would be getting into the Jeep on the left. But then his mouth softened into those dangerously sensual lines and he slid a hand around her neck, under her hair. Suddenly she couldn't think straight.

'If we don't do this…explore our mutual desire…it'll eat us up inside like acid. If you're strong enough to walk away, to deny this, then go ahead. I won't come after you, Sylvie. You'll never see me again.'

She wanted to pour scorn on Arkim's words. The sheer *arrogance*! As if she *wanted* to see him again! She should be pulling away from him and saying *good riddance*. But there was a quality to his voice… Something almost…rough. Pleading. And the thought of never seeing him again made her want to reach out and grip the material of his tunic in her fist. Not walk away.

God. What did that mean? What did that make *her*?

Arkim took his hand away and stepped back. Sylvie almost reached out for him. She teetered on the cliff-edge of a very scary and precipitous drop into the unknown. His words seduced her: *There are things about you that I don't know… that I want to know.*

A fluttering started low in her belly. Nerves, excitement. The thought of going with him…getting to know him more…letting him be intimate with her…was terrifying. But the thought of leaving… going back to her life and not knowing him…was more terrifying.

Sylvie's gut had been guiding her for a long time now—taking her out of the toxic orbit of her stepmother and her father's black grief at the age of seventeen—and it was guiding her towards the Jeep on the right-hand side before she could stop herself.

Arkim displayed no discernible triumph or sanctimony. He just held the passenger door open for her to get in, closed it, and got in at the other side. Sylvie was aware of the staff re-materialising, to put their bags in the back of the Jeep, and once that was done Arkim was pulling away and out of the castle.

She tried to drum up a sense of shame for her easy capitulation but it eluded her. All she felt was a fizzing sense of illicit anticipation.

Endless rolling desert and blue skies surrounded them. It should have been a boring landscape but it wasn't. And the silence that enveloped them was surprisingly easy as Arkim navigated over a road that was little more than a dirt track.

Eventually, though, Sylvie had to say the words beating a tattoo in her brain. She looked at him, taking in his aristocratic profile. 'Halima told me you've never brought anyone else to the castle.'

His hands tightened on the steering wheel momentarily and his jaw twitched. 'No, I haven't taken anyone else there.'

She hated it that she cared, because it meant nothing, and the feeling of exposure after having mentioned it made her say frigidly, 'I should have guessed that you'd prefer to keep this…*situation* well out of the prying gaze of the media. The last thing you want is to be publicly associated with someone like *me*.'

Arkim glanced at Sylvie, and she was surprised to see his mouth tip up ever so slightly at one side. 'I think our association became pretty public when you broke apart the wedding and claimed that I'd spent the night in your bed.'

She flushed. She'd conveniently forgotten that. She never had been a good liar. Afraid he'd ask her again about her motive for doing such a thing, she said hurriedly, 'This oasis—it's yours?'

Arkim finally looked away again to the road— but not before Sylvie's skin had prickled hotly under his assessing gaze. 'Yes, it's part of the land I own. However, nomads and travellers use it, and

I would never disallow them access as some others do. It's really their land.'

There was unmistakable pride in Arkim's tone, and it made Sylvie realise that, whatever their tangled relationship was, this man was not without integrity.

Genuinely curious, she asked, 'What's your connection to Al-Omar?'

Arkim's jaw tightened. 'This is where my mother is from—hence my name. The land belonged to a distant ancestor. She grew up in B'harani; her father was an advisor to the old Sultan, before Sadiq took over.'

'And do you see any of your family here?'

Before he'd even answered Sylvie might have guessed the truth from the way his face became stern again.

'They disowned my mother when she brought shame on the family name—in their eyes. They've never expressed any interest in meeting me.'

Sylvie felt a surge of emotion and said quietly, 'I'm sorry that she had to go through that. She must have felt lonely.'

How bigoted and cruel of them, to just leave her. But she didn't think Arkim would appreciate any further discussion on the subject, or hearing her saying she felt sorry for him.

She looked out of the window and took the opportunity to move things on to a less contentious footing. 'It is beautiful here...so different to anything I've ever seen before.'

There was a mocking tone to his voice. 'You don't miss the shops? Clubs? Busy city life?'

She immediately felt defensive. 'I love living in Paris, yes. But I actually hate shopping. And I work late almost every night, so on the nights I *do* have off the last thing I want to do is go out to a club.'

Arkim seemed to consider this for a moment. Then he settled back into his seat and angled his body towards her, one hand relaxed on the wheel and the other on his thigh.

'So tell me something else about yourself, then... How did you end up in Paris at seventeen?'

Sylvie cursed herself. She'd asked for it, hadn't she? By changing the subject. She looked at him and there was something different about him— something almost conciliatory. As if he was making an effort.

Because he wants you in his bed.

She ignored the mocking voice. 'I left home at

seventeen because I was never the most academic student and I wanted to dance.'

She deliberately avoided going into any more detail.

'So why not dance in the UK? Why did you have to go to Paris? Surely your aspirations were a little higher?'

Arkim sounded genuinely mystified instead of condemning, and Sylvie felt a rush of emotion when she remembered those tumultuous days. Her hands clenched into fists in her lap without her realising what they were doing.

Suddenly one of his hands covered hers. He was frowning at her. 'What is it?'

Shocked at the gesture, she looked at him. The warmth of his hand made her speak without really thinking. 'I was just remembering... It was not...an easy time.'

Arkim took his hand away to put it on the wheel again, in order to navigate an uneven part of the road. When they were through it, he said, 'Go on.'

Sylvie faced forward, hands clasped tightly in her lap. She'd never spoken of this with anyone—not really. And to find that she was about to speak of it now, to this man, was a little mind-boggling.

Yet even *his* judgement could never amount to

the self-recrimination she felt for behaving so re-actively. Even though she couldn't really regret it. She'd learnt so much about herself in the process.

'As is pretty obvious, my stepmother and I don't get on. We never have since she married my fa-ther. And my father... Our relationship is strained. I rebelled quite a bit—against both of them. And Catherine, my stepmother, was making life...dif-ficult for me.'

'How?' Arkim's voice was sharp.

'She wanted me to be sent to a finishing school in Switzerland—a way to get rid of me. So I left. I went to Paris to find some old contacts of my mother's. I'd always wanted to dance, and I'd taken lessons as a child... But after my mother died my father lost interest. And when Cathe-rine came along she insisted that dance classes weren't appropriate. She had issues with keeping my mother's memory alive.'

That was putting it mildly. Her father had had issues too, and his had had more far-reaching con-sequences for Sylvie. Her stepmother was just a jealous, insecure woman. She'd never known Syl-vie well enough for her rejection to really hurt. But her father *had* known her.

'So you took off to Paris on your own and started working at the revue?'

Sylvie nodded and settled back into her seat, the luxurious confines of the vehicle making it seductively easy to relax a little more. 'I had about one hundred pounds in my pocket when I met up with Pierre and found a home at the revue. I had to pay my way, of course. He let me take dance classes, but only if I cleaned in my spare time.'

'You took no money from your father?'

Sylvie glanced at Arkim's frown and slightly incredulous expression and wondered why she was surprised at his assumption that she would have. 'No, I haven't taken a penny from my father since I left home. I'm very proud of the money I make—it's not much, but it's mine and it's hard-earned.'

He schooled his expression. This information put everything he knew about Sylvie on its head and pricked his conscience. It was so completely opposite to everything he'd always assumed about her: that she was a trust fund kid, petulant and bored, seeking to disgrace her family just because she could. It sounded as if she'd sought refuge in Paris out of rebellion, yes, but also because she'd more or less been pushed away.

Very aware of that direct gaze on him, he said a little gruffly, 'You should rest for a bit—it'll take another hour or so to get there.'

Sylvie's eyes flashed at his clear dismissal of the subject, but gradually the tense lines of her body relaxed and she curled her legs up on the seat. Her head drifted to one side, long red hair trailing down over her shoulder.

Her lashes were long and dark against her cheeks. She wore no make-up, and Arkim noticed a smattering of small, almost undetectable freckles across the bridge of her nose. Had that been the sun? Because he didn't remember seeing them before. They gave her an air of innocence that compounded the naivety he'd seen in her dancing.

His chest felt tight. He looked back to the desert road, feeling slightly panicked. He shouldn't have indulged his base desire like this. He'd already behaved completely out of character by bringing her to Al-Omar in the first place—like some medieval overlord. He should have called the helicopter and got them both back to civilisation. He'd made his point—he'd demonstrated his anger.

But his hands gripped the steering wheel tight and he kept on driving. Because he wasn't ready to call it quits, to let her go. And she'd made a very clear choice to stay, and the triumph he'd felt in that moment still beat in his blood. Why would he turn back now, when they could exorcise this lust between them and get on with their lives?

'We're here.'

Sylvie opened her eyes and looked out of her window, straightening up in her seat as wonder and awe filled her. Maybe she was still dreaming? Because this was paradise. They were surrounded by lush greenery—greener than anything she'd ever seen before.

Arkim had got out of the Jeep and was opening her door. She got out on wobbly legs, eyes on stalks.

Two big tents were set up nearby—dark and lavishly decorated, with their tops coming to a point in the centre. Smaller tents sat off at a distance, separated from the others by trees. Sand dunes rose up around the camp, almost encircling it on one side, and on the other side was a rocky wall. When Sylvie shaded her eyes to look, she saw the most exquisite natural pool.

She walked over, stunned. The water was so clear she could see right down to the rocks at the bottom. The air was warm and soft—a million miles from the harsh heat she'd experienced since she'd arrived.

She felt Arkim's presence beside her but was afraid to look at him because her emotions were all over the place—especially so soon after waking up. It was as if she was missing a layer of skin.

'This is obviously a very special place,' she finally managed to get out, without sounding too husky.

'Yes, it is. I think it's the most peaceful spot on this earth.'

Sylvie looked at him at last and saw that he was staring down into the water. When he lifted his head and looked at her his gaze was so direct that it took her breath away. It was the most unguarded she'd ever seen him, and she could see so many things in his eyes. But the one that hit her right in the belly was desire.

She had a feeling that whatever lay tangled between them—all the animosity, misjudgement and distrust—it was slipping away and becoming irrelevant. What was relevant was here and now. Just the two of them—a man and a woman.

It was so primal that Sylvie was almost taking a

step towards Arkim before she realised that someone was interrupting them, telling him something.

Arkim's gaze slipped from Sylvie's and she held herself rigid, aghast that she'd come so close to revealing herself like that. Was she really so ready to jump into his arms? Even though she'd already tacitly capitulated by coming here?

Sylvie composed herself as Arkim talked to the man, and then he was turning towards her. 'Lunch has been prepared for us.'

She welcomed the break in the heightened tension and followed him as he led her to an open area outside the tents, where a table had been set up under a fabric covering held up by four posts. It was rustic, but charming.

The table was low, covered in a deep red silk tablecloth, and there was no cutlery. Arkim indicated a big cushion on one side of the table for Sylvie and she sat down, mesmerised by the mouth-watering array of foods laid out on platters. The smell alone was enough to get her stomach growling.

Arkim settled himself opposite her and handed her a plate with an assortment of food which she surmised she was meant to eat with her hands. Silver finger bowls were set by their plates.

Sylvie experimented with something that looked like a rice ball, closing her eyes in appreciation as warm cheese melted into her mouth. When she opened them again she saw Arkim taking a sip of golden liquid and watching her. There was something very sensual about eating with her hands. And then she looked at Arkim's strong hands and imagined them tracing her body... Heat suffused her face.

'Try your drink—it's a special brew of the region. Not exactly wine, but a relation.'

Sylvie hurriedly took a sip, hoping it might cool her down. It was like nectar—sweet but with a tart finish. 'It's delicious.'

Arkim's mouth tipped up. 'It's also lethal, so just a few sips is enough.'

She frowned. 'I thought people didn't really drink in this part of the world?'

'They don't... But there are nomads from this region who have made a name for themselves with this brew. It's a secret recipe, handed down over hundreds of years and made from rare desert berries.'

Sylvie took another sip and relished the smooth glide of the cold liquid down her throat. She realised that she'd always known what sensuality was in an abstract and intellectual way, and that she could exude it when she wanted to, but she'd never really embodied it herself. She felt as if she embodied it now, though, when this man looked at her. Or touched her.

She put the glass down quickly, shocked at how easily this place was entrancing her. And at how easily Arkim was intriguing her by making her believe that things had somehow shifted. They had...but in essence nothing much had changed. She was who she was, and *he* was who he was.

When this man set his mind to seduction it was nigh impossible to resist him, and Sylvie had a sense that she was far more vulnerable to him than she even realised herself. She knew it was irrational, because she'd already agreed to come here, but she felt she had to push him back.

She heard herself saying, 'Why go to the trouble of bringing me here when we both know this isn't about romance? You say you don't hate me, but what you do feel for me isn't far off that.'

Arkim looked at Sylvie from where he lounged across the table. Her hair glowed so bright it almost hurt to look at. Her skin was like alabaster—like a pearl against the backdrop of this ochre-hued place.

He replied with an honesty he hadn't intended. 'You've turned my life upside down. You irritate me and frustrate me...and I want you more than I've ever wanted another woman. What I feel for you is...ambiguous.'

Sylvie looked at him, and this time there was no mistaking the hurt flashing in her eyes. Before Arkim could react she stood up and paced away for a moment, and then she swung round, hair slipping over one shoulder, tunic billowing around her feet.

She crossed her arms. 'This was a mistake. I should never have come here with you.'

Arkim cursed his mouth and surged to his feet. Yet again Sylvie was exposing all his most base qualities. He couldn't believe how uncouth he was around this woman. He moved towards her and she took a step back. He controlled his impulse to grab her.

'You're here because you want to be, Sylvie— plain and simple. This isn't about what's happened. This is about us—here and now. Nothing else. I won't dress it up in fancy language. There is a physical honesty between us which I believe has more integrity than any fluctuating and fickle emotions.'

He saw how she paled, but how her pulse stayed hectic. Arkim felt as if he held the most delicate of brightly coloured humming-birds in his palm and it was about to fly away, never to be seen again.

He wanted her full acquiescence—for her to admit she wanted him. It unnerved him how much he wanted that when he hadn't given much consideration to her feelings before now.

Another truth forced its way out. 'You were right last night. I don't know you, but I want to. Sit down...finish eating. Please.'

Arkim was tense, waiting. But eventually Sylvie moved jerkily and sat down again. None of her usual grace was evident. She avoided his eyes as he took his seat again and they ate some more, awareness and tension crackling between them like a live wire.

After a minute she wiped her mouth with a napkin and took another sip of her drink. Then she looked at Arkim, her blue-green gaze disturbingly intense.

'So...what was it like growing up in LA?'

Relief that she was engaging stripped away Arkim's guardedness. His inner reaction to her question was a list of words. *Brash. Artificial. Ex-*

cessive. But he said, 'I hated it. So much so that I've never been back.'

Sylvie assimilated that, and then said, 'I've been to Las Vegas and I hated it there. It's so fake—like a film set.'

A spurt of kinship surprised Arkim. 'LA is massive—sprawling. Lots of different areas separated by miles of freeway...no real connection. Everyone is looking for a place in the spotlight—striving to be skinnier, more tanned, more perfect than the next person. There's no soul.'

'They say no one walks in LA.'

Arkim smiled and it felt odd—because he wasn't used to smiling so spontaneously in the presence of anyone, much less a woman.

'That's true. Unless you go somewhere like Santa Monica, and then it's like a catwalk.'

'You really haven't seen your father since you left?'

He shook his head. 'Not since I was seventeen.' Then he grimaced. 'That's not entirely accurate. I would have left voluntarily, but I was still too young. He threw me out.'

'Why?'

Arkim steeled himself. 'Because he caught me having sex with his mistress—a famous porn actress.'

He saw myriad expressions cross Sylvie's face: shock, hurt, and then anger.

She put her napkin down, eyes flaming, jaw tight. 'You absolute hypocrite! You have the gall to subject me to your judge and jury act and all the time—'

'Wait.' Arkim's voice rang out harshly.

He hadn't even been aware of the impulse to lean across the table and capture Sylvie's wrist in his hand before he realised that was what he was doing. Panic made his gut clench. For the first time in his life he found that his words were tripping out before he could stop them—along with an urge to make her understand.

Because if Sylvie damned him then there truly was no hope for his redemption at all...

'I didn't seduce her. She seduced me.'

Sylvie looked at Arkim, her wrist still caught in his firm grip. There was something almost desperate in his eyes. Her anger, which had flared so quickly, started to fizzle out. 'What do you mean?'

He let her wrist go and stood up, moving away from the table to pace, running a hand through his hair. Sylvie had never seen him like this. On the edge of his control.

He turned to face her, his face etched in stark lines. 'I was back from England for the summer holidays. My father had refused to let me stay in Europe for the summer, even though I'd offered to pay my own way by working. I'd done my A levels. I was just biding my time until I had to go to college. My father knew I hated LA, so he taunted me with it.'

His mouth twisted. 'Cindy was everywhere I was. Especially when my father wasn't around. And invariably she was half-naked.'

Self-disgust was evident in his voice.

'I thought I could resist her...I tried for the whole summer. I was only a few days from returning to the UK and she found me by the pool. I was too weak. The worst thing was that she stayed in control the whole time while I lost it. My father found us in the pool house.'

He didn't have to elaborate on what had happened next for Sylvie to join the dots. She shouldn't be feeling anything other than what he'd dished out to her—judgement and condemnation... But she couldn't help it. Sympathy surged in her breast. She could well imagine that whatever judgement she might hurl at Arkim, he'd already judged himself a thousand times over—and far more harshly than anyone else could have.

'You were seventeen, Arkim. There's probably not a straight teenage hormonal boy on the planet who could have resisted the seduction of an older and more experienced woman—much less a porn star whose job is controlling sex.'

Arkim's harsh lines didn't relax. 'She only did it because she wanted to make my father jealous... to push him into some kind of commitment. She gambled the wrong way, though. He threw her out too.'

He turned away from her then, to look out at the view. His back was broad, formidable. As if he didn't want her to look at him.

'Do you know I saw my first orgy when I was eight?'

Sylvie put a hand to her mouth, glad he wasn't looking at her reaction. She took her hand down after a moment. 'Arkim...that's—'

He turned around again. He was harsh. 'That was my life. Someone saw me watching, and of course I couldn't really understand what was happening. It was after that that my father sent me to school in England. He got off on the idea of sending me to school with English royalty. But it saved me, I think. I only had to survive the holidays, and I learned to avert my eyes from the debauched parties he liked to throw.'

The thought of such a small child witnessing such things and then being sent away... Sylvie stood up. 'That was abuse, Arkim. And what that woman did to you—seducing you like that—it was a form of abuse too.'

Arkim smiled, but it was infinitely cynical and Sylvie suddenly loathed it.

'*Was* it abuse? When it was the most exciting moment of my life at that point? She showed me how much pleasure a man can feel. I submitted to her. Even though I hated myself for it.'

For a second Sylvie felt a blinding flash of jealousy so acute she nearly gasped. The thought of this man being helpless, submitting to a woman who had given him pleasure...and who was not *her*...was painful.

Thankfully he didn't seem to notice her seismic reaction and he said, 'Do you know what it's like to grow up under the influence of someone with no moral compass?'

Sylvie shook her head, clawing back control.

He was grim. 'It's like you're tainted by his

deeds—no matter what you do to try and distance yourself. It's a tattoo on your skin—for ever. And I failed the test. I proved I was no better than my father—a man who debased a sweet, innocent woman from a foreign country and all but dumped her by the road when she needed him most.'

His words sank heavily into the silence, and just like that Sylvie saw Arkim's intense personal struggle. Saw why he'd always reacted so strongly to her. She understood now how very attractive a respectable marriage would be—it would offer him everything he'd never had. It all made sense. And her heart ached.

The approach of another staff member broke the bubble surrounding them. The man said something to Arkim that Sylvie couldn't understand. She was reeling with all this new information, feeling such a mix of things that she hardly knew how to assimilate it all.

The man left and Arkim turned to her, his face expressionless again, as if he *hadn't* just punched a hole in her chest with his revelations.

'There are some nomads who want to meet with me. You should rest for a while—it's the hottest part of the day.'

Sylvie felt his dismissal like a glancing blow,

but before she could say a word Arkim was strid-
ing away. A middle-aged woman dressed all in
black appeared by her side. She had a smiling face
and kind eyes. She said something Sylvie couldn't
understand and gestured for Sylvie to follow her.
With no other choice, she did, and was led to the
smaller of the two big tents.

The woman slipped off her shoes before she
went in so Sylvie copied her, not wanting to cause
any offence.

It took her eyes a moment to adjust to the darker
interior, and when they had her jaw dropped. It
was refreshingly cooler inside, and the entire
floor area was covered in oriental rugs, each in a
more lavish design than the last. Her toes curled
at the sensation of the expensive material under
her feet…it was like silk.

The tent was simply the most decadent thing
Sylvie had ever seen. Dark and full of lustrous
materials. Huge soft cushions around a low coffee table; a dressing screen with intricate Chi-
nese drawings. Beautiful lamps threw out soft
lights…drawing the eye to the most focal point
of the tent: the bed.

It was on a raised platform in the centre of the
room. It was a four-poster, with heavy drapes

pulled back at each corner. More cushions in lush jewel colours were strewn artfully across the pillows, and the sheets—Sylvie reached out to touch them—they were made of satin and silk. The bed was a byword in shameless opulence.

Sylvie caught the older woman's eye. She was looking at her with a very knowing glint. There was obviously only one reason for Sylvie to be here with the Sheikh.

She blushed furiously, squirming on the spot, and suffered through being shown the bathroom—another eye-poppingly sensual space, complete with a huge copper claw-footed bath—and tried not to die of embarrassment.

When the woman had left, Sylvie paced back and forth, expecting to see Arkim darken the tent's doorway at any moment. She felt panic at the thought of seeing him again. When he didn't appear she sank down into a chair near the bottom of the bed and glared balefully at the entrance of the tent for a few minutes. She realised that Arkim had really meant her to have a nap. He wasn't coming.

A sense of disappointment cut through all the other emotions, mocking her. The last thing she felt like doing was napping—she was so keyed up, her mind racing. But when she got up and sat down on the edge of the sumptuous bed it seemed to draw her into the centre, cushioning her like a cloud.

The last thing she remembered before sleep claimed her was vowing to herself that she would absolutely *not* think again about what he'd just told her—because that way lay all sorts of danger, and feelings that made her far too susceptible to the man.

CHAPTER SEVEN

SYLVIE WOKE SOME time later with a jolt. She'd been having a horrible dream about hundreds of naked faceless people with bare limbs entwined— so much so that she couldn't tell where one person ended and another began. She was tiny in the dream, and trying to find a way out, but gradually getting more and more suffocated...

She scowled and stretched out her stiff limbs. So much for not thinking about what Arkim had told her. She shook off the disturbing tendrils of the dream and looked around, taking in the fact that someone must have come into the tent and lit some more lights. *Arkim?* The thought made her heart beat faster.

She went into the bathing area and, feeling sticky, took off her clothes and dropped them to the floor. She stepped under the shower, which was in a large private cubicle near the bath and open to the elements. Twilight was just starting to turn the sky dusky, and Sylvie couldn't help but be affected by the magic of the place as the deliciously warm water sluiced down over her head and body.

Eventually she switched off the shower, dragged a towel around herself and twisted up her damp hair. She found a robe hanging on the back of the dressing screen. It was a beautiful emerald-green colour, silk—light as a feather. Slipping it on, she relished its coolness against her skin.

And then she went to the door of the tent and looked out. Twilight was descending around the camp in earnest now, bathing it in a gorgeous lilac light. She didn't see anyone moving, but could hear low voices in the distance and smell something cooking. No sign of Arkim. She didn't like the hollow feeling that brought with it. Only a couple of hours ago she'd been ready to leave, and then he'd told her...so much.

She thought of the pool she'd seen when they'd arrived and slipped her shoes on to explore. The air was sultry and warm, even though the intensity of the day had diminished. When she came close to the beautifully peaceful pool she pushed aside foliage and then she stopped dead in her tracks, her heart in her mouth, because it was occupied.

By a butt-naked Arkim.

He stood in the shallows, and all she could see were the firm globes of a very muscular bottom as he bent and threw water over his head. Water ran in rivulets down his back. And then he stood straight and tensed. He'd sensed her. Sylvie stopped breathing. She knew she should turn and run. Do something. But she couldn't move.

And then he turned around.

His hair was slicked back, and he was...*magnificent*. Sylvie had seen plenty of naked male bodies—working at the revue and helping people change between numbers meant personal modesty quickly became a thing of the past. But she'd never seen a man like this. He looked as if he'd been carved out of rock. His chest was broad and leanly muscled. His chest hair was dark and dusted over his pectorals before dissecting his chest and abs to lead down to slim hips and...

Sylvie's heart was beating so fast she wasn't sure how she was still standing. Arkim's penis twitched under her gaze, the shaft getting harder as she watched, rising from the thicket of dark hair between his powerfully muscled thighs.

Somehow she dragged her gaze up and his dark

eyes were on her, molten... The very air seemed to contract around them.

When she'd first seen him he'd been dressed in that three-piece suit, all buttoned up. Here, now, he was stripped bare. Without the armour that told the world he was different, respectable. To Sylvie there was something very poignant about finding Arkim like this, naked.

He stepped out of the pool and gracefully bent down to pick up a piece of material and wrap it around his waist. Sylvie was barely aware. Her entire body and mind was focused solely on this man, on this moment. It throbbed with potential.

She realised with a stunning flash of clarity that she wanted to give herself to him—this man who had never had a moment of purity in his life. Who'd seen things at a young age that had darkened his view of the world for ever.

It was the one thing she had—her innocence. And with every fibre of her being she wanted to gift it to *him*. As if she could assuage the raw edges she'd seen earlier.

Arkim walked up to her and Sylvie's eyes stayed on his, unblinking. She was drawing confidence from his obvious arousal and his intentness on her.

He looked almost ferocious, every line of his body and face unyielding. 'What do you want, Sylvie?'

It wasn't just a question. It was almost a demand.

Sylvie spoke what was in her heart and soul. And in her body. 'I want *you*, Arkim.'

He came closer and lifted a hand, undoing the pin holding up her damp hair, letting it fall loose around her shoulders. He put his hands on her arms and pulled her closer. Closer to that bare wet chest. Until they were touching. Until the points of her breasts hurt with the need to press against him more fully. His erection pushed against her lower belly and excitement flooded her, making her ready.

'Arkim...' she said, not even sure what she was asking for. Why wasn't he taking her right now? Making the most of his conquering?

'You're sure you want this?'

Sylvie hadn't been expecting this consideration. Another dangerously tender emotion ran through her. She didn't hesitate. She moved closer, feeling the delicious press of her breasts against him. 'Yes.'

Just one word. Simple, but devastating.

In a rush of emotion she said, 'I want to give

you—' But she stopped, not sure how to articulate exactly what she *did* want to give him. So she just said a little lamely, 'I want to give you myself.'

Arkim's hands were so tight on her arms it almost hurt, but then they relaxed marginally and he bent down for a moment. She felt herself being lifted into his arms, against his chest, and he walked back the way she'd come.

One of her arms was tight around his neck and she ducked her head into his chest, eyes shut tight. Her other hand was on her robe, holding it together. She didn't want to catch the knowing eyes of that woman, or anyone else. She felt too raw and needy.

And also dangerously cossetted, held in his arms like this.

She pushed down all the tangled emotional implications of how she was feeling and focused on the urgent hunger racing through her blood.

When everything felt cooler and darker Sylvie knew that they'd entered an interior space and opened her eyes again. It had to be Arkim's tent—similar to hers, but bigger, more masculine, with bolder colours. And the bed in the centre of the tent was…huge.

Arkim carried her over and put her down on her

feet by the side of it. She avoided looking at it by looking at him.

He cupped her face with his hand. 'I've wanted you from the moment I saw you. I saw it as a weakness, as something to be denied...but not any more.'

Sylvie felt vulnerable. She believed him, and his words had all sorts of implications she couldn't think about right now.

Acting on impulse, she raised herself on tiptoe and put her arms around his neck. 'Stop talking... you're ruining the moment.'

Arkim smiled, and it was devilish. It made something soar inside her.

He tugged the belt on Sylvie's robe and it fell open. She unwrapped her arms from his neck and stood before him, heart palpitating wildly as Arkim pushed the robe apart, revealing her naked body to his dark gaze.

He looked at her for a long moment, until Sylvie could start to feel herself trembling lightly. She was someone who knew her own body intimately, as any dancer would, but right now it felt foreign, and she was insecure.

'You're shaking.'

She looked at him and tried a smile. 'You're quite intimidating.'

Arkim's answer to that was to take off the material around his waist before he pushed her robe off her shoulders so that it fell down her arms and to the floor.

'Now we're equal.'

Those words impacted deep inside her. All along she'd fought a battle with this man not to let him make her feel inferior, less than him. The moment was heady.

Arkim turned then, taking her with him as he moved closer to the bed. Sylvie was unbalanced and fell against him, but he caught her easily and drew her down with him, so they landed on the soft surface in a sprawl of limbs.

She was lying on top of his hard body, every inch of her flesh coming into contact with his. She felt dizzy. And then Arkim's hands were smoothing down her bare back and cupping her buttocks, pulling her thighs apart so that they lay either side of his hips.

His mouth reached up to hers and Sylvie felt her hair fall over her shoulders, screening them as she fell into the kiss…wet and rough and intoxicating.

After more long, languorous kisses Arkim

moved, so that Sylvie was now the one on her back, and he loomed over her, huge and awe-inspiring in the gloom of the tent. One of his thighs was between her legs and he moved it against her, making her body twitch and ache. The friction caused a delicious tension to coil inside her and she bit her lip.

Arkim's gaze roved over her body hungrily. 'You are more beautiful than I could ever have imagined.'

Sylvie shook her head, feeling breathless because of what was happening between her legs. 'No...*you're* beautiful.'

But he didn't seem to be listening. He was transfixed by her breasts, cupping one now, so that the hard point pouted upwards wantonly. He lowered his head and blew gently on it, making her tingle and ache for more, and then his mouth was on her, and that wicked tongue, flicking and sucking on the turgid flesh.

Her hands were in his hair, fingers funnelling deep, holding him to her. Her back was arched and she was fast losing any sense of reason. Or maybe she'd lost it when she'd laid eyes on this man for the first time. Anyway, it was gone.

He lavished attention on both breasts until they

ached and felt swollen, and then his mouth was moving down…over her belly and lower. Sylvie only realised her hands were still on his head when he reached up to take them away. Taking both her hands in one of his, he held them captive over her belly.

Now she really was at his mercy. He moved lower, the bulk of his body forcing her legs apart.

Sylvie lifted her head and looked down. 'Arkim…' Her voice sounded rough, broken. Taut with need.

He looked up at her and said, 'Shh…'

Sylvie's head was too heavy. She let it fall back just as he released her hands, and then both of his hands were on her buttocks, lifting her to his mouth, where his tongue explored the damp folds of her sex, laying her so open she couldn't bear it.

She had to bite down on a fist when she felt his tongue surge deep inside her, and then his teeth were nipping… The tension was coiling so tightly now she thought she might have to scream to release the pressure, and he was relentless.

Sylvie was vaguely aware of bucking towards him mindlessly—and then he reached up and squeezed her breast, and she exploded into a million tiny pieces of pleasure so intense that she couldn't breathe or see.

She'd orgasmed before—you couldn't work in her industry and remain completely unaware of taking pleasure—but it had always been by her own hand, and never this...*mind-blowing*. She'd actually thought it was overrated. Evidently she'd been doing it all wrong, she thought dreamily as her body floated back to earth slowly, lusciously.

She was aware of him moving aside momentarily, with an intense focus in his movements, and then he was back, coming over her and leaning on both arms, the muscles bunched and taut.

Sylvie felt him lodge himself between her legs, and then the potent thrust of his erection against the sensitised folds of her sex. For a moment she thought it might be too soon, that she couldn't possibly— But then he hitched himself against her, the head of his erection sliding tantalisingly between those folds, and her whole body quivered with anticipation.

Instinctively she put her hands on Arkim's arms, as if to hold on for the ride, and her legs opened wider in tacit acceptance.

Sylvie's eyes were huge, staring up at him as if he knew all the secrets of the universe. Arkim didn't know how he hadn't already spilled onto the sheets, like the virginal teenager he'd been all those years ago, when he'd felt her body convulse in spasms of pleasure. But somehow he hadn't... and now he was on the very edge of his control as he felt her body accept his.

He started to sink into her tight, silken hot sheath.

Her *very* hot and *very* tight sheath.

In fact as Arkim's body sought to go deeper he realised that Sylvie's body was tight against him in a way he'd never encountered before...

His brain was overheating, his body screaming for a release of the tension, and those huge limpid eyes were still staring up at him. The hard tips of her breasts scraping against his chest.

Arkim was about to lose it...the heady scent of musk and sex urged him on. He gritted his jaw and thrust hard—and went nowhere.

He heard Sylvie's swift, sharp intake of breath and looked down. His brain was feeling too hot, too fuzzy to try and figure out what was wrong. But something *was* wrong. Very wrong.

Moments ago Sylvie had been flushed with pleasure. Now she looked pale and clammy. Shocked. She was biting her lip and her eyes shone with...*tears*?

Arkim's insides seemed to drop from a height. But even as suspicion crept in he fought the knowledge... She was just small—that was it. A lot smaller than he'd realised she was.

He clenched his buttocks, trying to forge a passage, and Sylvie's hands gripped his like steel clamps, her nails digging into his muscles.

'Stop—please! It *hurts.*'

And the truth resounded in Arkim's head like a klaxon going off. *Virgin. Innocent.*

It was too much to take in. But he had to. *She was a virgin.*

Arkim pulled back from Sylvie's resisting body, her wince of obvious pain making him feel as if someone had just punched him in the gut. Somehow he got off the bed, stood up... His legs were shaky. He stared at Sylvie but didn't really see her, and then he acted on autopilot, going to the bathing area to take care of the protection.

He caught the expression on his face in the mirror and stopped. He looked dark, feral. He looked...*like his father.* With that insatiable glint in his eye. Narcissistic and intent only on his own self-satisfaction. Uncaring if someone might be innocent, pure. Like his mother. *Like Sylvie.*

He was no better than his father. This proved it

more than any teenage humiliation with a porn actress. Something cold settled down over Arkim's heart. Something hard and familiar.

He went back out to the main area of the tent and saw Sylvie sitting on the side of the bed, the sheet wrapped around her body. She looked at him over her shoulder and the dark hardness inside Arkim nearly split apart because she looked so forlorn.

He reached for his trousers and pulled them on, irrational anger growing deep down inside him and crawling upwards to catch him in its hot grip.

'Why didn't you tell me?' He walked around to stand in front of her.

She looked shell-shocked. Arkim drove the emotion down.

'Why?' It burst out of him like the firing of a rifle.

Sylvie flinched, her hands clutching the sheet to her chest. 'I wasn't sure you'd notice. I almost told you...but I didn't know how.'

Arkim felt as if all of his ugliness was exposed. He sneered. 'How about, *Hey, Arkim, I'm a virgin, by the way...be gentle with me.*'

Sylvie stood up then, and Arkim could see how she trembled. The exposed skin of her shoulder and upper chest was very white. Delicate. Fragile. And he'd been like a rutting bull in a china shop.

He wanted to smash something.

'I didn't think you'd notice and I didn't think it was important.'

'Well, I *did* notice and it *is* important.' Arkim stalked away and then back, folding his arms across his chest. 'You're twenty-eight and you work in a strip club—how the hell are you still a virgin?'

Sylvie hitched her chin. 'It's *not* a strip club. And I just...was never interested before now.'

She started to look around for her things and Arkim caught her by the arm. The anger inside him was a turbulent mass. Everything in him wanted to lash out, to blame someone—blame *her*. If she'd told him...

What? asked a snide voice. *Would you have let her go?*

Never.

'Why, Sylvie? And it's not just because you weren't interested. You're a sexual being—it oozes from you. I had no idea. If I had—'

She wrenched her arm free, fire flashing in her eyes now, any hint of vulnerability gone. 'You'd have what? Declined the offer?'

She spied her robe on the ground and grabbed it, letting the sheet fall as she tugged it on—but not before Arkim saw that luscious body and his own reacted forcibly.

Then she stopped and glared at him. 'You want to know the psychological motivation behind my still being a virgin? Really?'

Suddenly he didn't. But she went on.

'My father rejected me as a child. My mother had died—his beloved wife—and I resembled her so much that he couldn't bear to look at me. So he sent me away. He's never been able to look at me since then without pain or grief. The truth is he would have switched me for her any day of the week.'

Arkim's chest ached. 'How can you know that?'

'Because I overheard him talking to someone. I heard him say how he couldn't bear the sight of me—that I was a constant reminder that she was gone and that if he could he'd have her back instead of me.'

Arkim reached out, but she slapped his hand away.

'And as for why I decided to let you be my first lover...? Well, maybe I felt bizarrely secure in the fact that you'd already rejected me on pretty much every level that counts. When you've protected yourself against rejection your whole life, it's almost a relief not to have to fear it any more.'

She stepped back, the robe pulled so tightly around her that every curve was lovingly delineated, and then she left.

Sylvie was so angry and humiliated she could have cried. But her anger kept the tears at bay. What on earth had possessed her to spill her soul to Arkim like that? As if he cared about the sob story of her relationship with her father. Or about her deepest inner fears of being rejected. She'd never even spoken to Sophie of any of this, not wanting to burden her sister with a negative view of their father.

Sylvie paced back and forth, her emotions vying between humiliation and anger, very aware of the dull throb and stinging between her legs. She stopped in her tracks when she thought of the excruciating pain of Arkim trying to penetrate her—his shock when he'd realised why he couldn't.

She sat down gingerly on the side of her own bed. She'd never expected it to be that bad. Up till that moment it had been the most incandescently pleasurable experience of her life. And she'd truly thought that he wouldn't know—that it would always be her own secret.

The tender feelings that had led Sylvie to want to soothe him in some way mocked her now. All the while she'd been thinking she was giving Arkim the supreme gift of her innocence he'd been ready to reject it outright. Evidently her lack of experience was a huge turn-off.

What she'd told Arkim wasn't entirely true— his outright rejection of her hadn't really prepared her for this. Or for how much it would hurt. Far more than the physical pain.

She reminded herself that she'd knowingly risked this when she'd chosen to come here. She had no one to blame but herself. It wasn't a comfort.

Arkim was undoubtedly done with her and his little plan of retribution. He would let her go and she would never see him again.

Feeling raw and weary, Sylvie stood and picked up her bag, started to fill it with the clothes that must have been unpacked when she'd been sleeping. She couldn't see Arkim doing such a menial task, so it hadn't been him in her tent.

Now she felt doubly foolish.

Packing her things with more force than necessary, Sylvie didn't hear anything until a deep and infinitely familiar voice spoke from behind her.

'What are you doing?'

Sylvie's entire body hummed in response. She cursed her reaction and didn't turn around. 'I'm leaving—what does it look like?'

'Why?'

There was some note in Arkim's voice that made her insides flutter dangerously but she ignored it. She steeled herself and dropped the clothes from her hands and turned around. In the dim flickering lights of the tent Arkim looked huge. He'd put a tunic on over his trousers.

'Your reaction just now was hardly indicative of wanting us to spend more time together.'

She thought Arkim winced, but couldn't be sure it wasn't a trick of the light and her imagination.

Then he said, 'I could have handled that better. Did I hurt you?' His voice had turned gruff.

The fluttering in her belly intensified, but Sylvie pushed it down ruthlessly. 'I'm okay.'

And she was. As soon as he'd pulled out the pain had faded and all that was left was some tenderness.

Then she said tartly, 'You obviously weren't prepared for me to be a virgin because all along you've assumed I'm some kind of a sl—'

'Do *not* even say that word.' Arkim stepped forward, the lines in his face harsh.

The hurt was back and more painful. Why was he doing this? Bothering? Sylvie crossed her arms, wishing she'd had the foresight to change out of the robe, which felt very flimsy now.

'Look, you don't have to do this...apologise, or whatever it is you're doing. I get it. Me being a virgin was not a welcome surprise, and I understand that you have no desire to be the one to initiate me.'

Arkim came closer and shook his head, a look of incredulity coming over his face. It was only now that she noticed the growth of stubble on his jaw, remembered how it had felt against her softer skin...*between her thighs*.

'That's not it at all. I didn't handle my reaction well and I'm sorry for that. I had no right to take out my anger on you. It was just a shock when I expected—' Arkim stopped and ran a hand through his hair and stepped back. He cursed and walked to the door of the tent.

For a heart-stopping second Sylvie thought he was leaving, and her brave façade was just about to crumble when he stopped and put his hand up over the top of the doorway.

He spoke into the inky darkness outside. 'My mother was a virgin. My father seduced her and took her virginity from her. She didn't even enjoy the experience. He was rough...'

Arkim turned around and Sylvie felt her heart beating too fast. She sank down onto the bed. 'How can you know this?'

He was grim. 'She kept a diary. It was in a box of her personal items that my father somehow miraculously kept. I read it when I was a teenager.' His voice was rough. 'When it became obvious you were...innocent I realised that I was doing to another woman exactly what he'd done to her.'

Sylvie shook her head and stood up again, compelled to go over to Arkim with a fierceness she'd never felt before. 'You didn't know...I could have explained, but I didn't.' She bit her lip. 'This is going to sound really stupid, but when you told me about what had happened to you...I wanted you to be the one...'

Arkim reared back slightly. 'You wanted to sleep with me because you felt sorry for me?'

'No.' She stopped, and then admitted sheepishly, 'Maybe, in a way...'

Arkim looked ready to bolt, but Sylvie put a hand on his arm. He stopped, his face etched with injured pride.

'Not like that.' Her mouth twitched slightly. 'Believe me, you don't inspire *pity* in people, Arkim—anything but. I wanted to sleep with you because you truly are the first person who has connected with me on that level... From the moment I saw you, I wanted you. Even when you looked at me with disdain it made me want to make you notice me.'

'I noticed you...' His tone was wry.

Sylvie's cheeks grew hot as she remembered that first time they'd met. The erroneous impression she'd made.

She let his arm go and shrugged lightly, avoided his eye. 'I thought that I could somehow gift you something...pure. The purest thing I have to give. To show you that not everything is tainted.' She looked at him again. 'You are nothing like your father. And I am nothing like your mother. This is *not* the same. You are considerate...you stopped when you knew I was in pain. It sounds like your father wasn't even aware of that.'

Something in the air between them changed... sizzled. The tension shifted to one full of awareness. Wanting.

Arkim lifted a hand and cupped Sylvie's jaw. 'What do you say we start again?'

Her breath hitched. Start again...? As in from the beginning or just from tonight? But she was too afraid to ask it out loud, to break this fragile spell. She'd bared herself completely to him and he was still here. Still wanted her.

'Yes...' she breathed.

Arkim moved closer and Sylvie's skin tingled all over. Her breasts, still sensitive, peaked to hard points.

'And, for the record, I don't reject you...I absolutely accept you.' His voice became fervent. 'You are *mine*, Sylvie. No one else's on this earth.' Something dark crossed his face. 'If I was a better man I'd let you go, but I'm too selfish to let anyone else have you.'

And then he kissed her, before she could say a word, and there was nowhere left to run or hide.

The fire swept up around them faster than before, and then he was carrying Sylvie over to the bed, putting her down and sweeping her clothes and bag away with one hand.

He took off his clothes and her hungry gaze roved over him, as if it was her first time seeing him. His erection strained from his body, thick and long. She felt a glimmer of fear, remembering the pain.

But as if reading her mind Arkim came down over her and said, 'I'll make it good...don't worry. It won't hurt again.'

She looked at him and felt her heart turn over. The thought of this man not taking the opportunity to hurt her...she'd never expected it. She couldn't speak. So she just nodded.

He carefully opened her robe and peeled it off her, laying her bare. And then he came alongside her on the bed and proceeded to do everything he'd done before, and more, until Sylvie was writhing, begging... Her sex was hot and damp, aching to feel him again, pain be damned.

'Touch me first,' he said hoarsely, poised above her, his powerful body between her legs.

Sylvie was nearly incoherent, her vision blurry. She looked down to see Arkim's sheathed erection and put a hand down to encircle him. She lamented the protection—she wanted to feel him skin to skin—but even like this…it was awe-inspiring. *He* was awe-inspiring.

She squeezed him gently, moved her hand up and down experimentally, and then she looked at him and saw the huge strain on his face. He was holding back, going slowly for her. Letting her get used to him.

Tenderness welled inside her. She took her hand from him and then placed both her hands on his hips, drawing her legs up in an instinctive feminine move as old as time.

'Now, Arkim—I need you now.'

She saw him struggle, and then give in. His body fused with hers and inch by inch he slowly sank into her. To the point of resistance.

'Sweetheart, relax…let me in.'

The endearment made something melt inside Sylvie and she could feel all the muscles that were clamping so hard against him relax.

Arkim slid a little deeper. She felt so full…almost uncomfortable. But also…*amazing.* Arkim kept going until Sylvie could barely breathe and his hips touched hers. She felt impaled…but *whole.* It was such a new and alien sensation. And then he started to pull out, beginning a dance of movement between their bodies that Sylvie had never known existed. Just when she thought he was withdrawing from her completely he'd thrust back in, and each time it felt a little more imperative that he did so.

Her legs were wrapped around his waist and her hands were on his buttocks now, silently commanding his movements to be stronger, more forceful.

Arkim huffed out laboured-sounding words. 'Should have known you'd be a fast learner...'

Sylvie smiled up at him—but then her smile got stuck as Arkim touched something deep inside her that sent shockwaves and thrills through her. His movements became faster, wilder, as if he couldn't control them any more, and the delicious tension Sylvie had felt before coiled tight within her again, and tighter. Until she begged for release.

Arkim put a hand between them and pressed his thumb against her, and Sylvie couldn't hold back her cry as she broke into shards of light and sensation. Her whole body convulsed with pleasure around Arkim's, her skin damp and slick.

Powerful shudders shook Arkim's body as he finally took his own release, and through the cataclysm Sylvie could feel the contractions of her body around his. In that moment she'd never felt so complete.

CHAPTER EIGHT

SYLVIE FLOATED ON her back, naked in the warm water, and looked up into an endless violet-hued sky. Early evening was practically the only time Arkim would let her out, for fear of the sun damaging her skin, even though she faithfully slathered on factor fifty.

The silky water lapped between her legs. Soothing the tenderness. She couldn't keep back a small smile... The last week had been the most illuminating, mind-blowing week of her life. It had been an intense tutorial in the sensual arts, with a master teacher.

She'd never known... She'd heard people talk about it, but had never really understood just what they'd been going on about. And that deep-rooted fear of rejection had made her shy away from any intimacy.

Not here, though. Every night and most of the day Arkim laid Sylvie bare, over and over again, until she was reduced to a mass of sensation and lusting and craving—no longer a human being. He'd turned her into some kind of animal.

That thought made something tighten inside her and Sylvie flipped over, lazily swimming to the far end of the pool. She wasn't worried about being seen—the staff knew not to come to the pool at this time, and used it only during the day.

She sat on a natural stone ledge in the water, the tops of her breasts exposed, and blushed when she imagined Arkim taking her here—pressing between her legs, urging her to wrap them around his waist as he thrust so deep inside her she'd have to bite down on his skin to contain her cries of ecstasy.

She wasn't entirely sure someone hadn't slipped a drug into her drink or food, and that this wasn't all some kind of crazy hallucination. But the air was warm on her wet skin, and the water was real enough. As was the smell of cooking. And the sounds of people in the distance, laughing and talking softly.

Sylvie hadn't seen much of the nomads—they kept themselves to themselves. And anyway... how could she notice anyone else when Arkim filled her vision larger than a twenty-foot statue?

Physically Sylvie had never been more replete or

happy. Emotionally, however... Her insides tightened again.

Since she and Arkim had started sleeping together there had been no more intensely personal
confessionals. She had no idea what he thought of
her now, beyond the very physical evidence that
he wanted her. And she wanted him. *Oh, God.*
She wanted him more and more each day. As if
the more she had of him the tighter would be the
bonds holding them together.

For her.

Sylvie knew one thing: even though he'd said
he accepted her, this was a moment out of time
for Arkim. He didn't have to say it. Whatever he'd
once thought of her—and whatever he thought of
her now—was irrelevant. This was just a slaking
of lust for him. And when they left here he would
turn his back and walk away. Because a man like
Arkim Al-Sahid, with all his dark secrets and
troubled past, would never choose a woman like
Sylvie.

Even if she *had* been a virgin, and that had
changed his perception of her, she was still unpalatable in his real world. Sylvie had to remember that, and not get caught up in this interim
magic and madness.

In spite of everything that had brought them here he'd given her an incredible gift. The gift of her own sensuality and sexuality. Which was ironic, considering she'd been successfully projecting it for years. He'd taken the broken pieces inside her and forged a new wholeness. And that was what she would take with her when this was over...

She heard a movement and looked up to see Arkim standing at the edge of the pool, with only a towel around his waist. Hair slicked back. He'd obviously just showered. Instantly Sylvie could feel the effect of his presence on her body—blood flowing to erogenous zones, flesh swelling, tingling, becoming engorged.

With his hands on his hips and a scowl on his face he looked truly intimidating. He was looking for her, and Sylvie's breath quickened as his gaze came closer and closer... *Zing!* Eye contact. Heat. Pulsing awareness.

The scowl faded and was replaced by a look of carnal intent. With one hand Arkim undid the towel and twitched it to the ground. He stepped into the pool—gloriously, unashamedly naked.

Like a little wanton, Sylvie had her legs open and ready for him when he came close enough to touch her. He registered her acquiescence with a feral smile that curled her insides.

The head of his erection notched against her sex, slipping between slick folds. His hands cupped and moulded her breasts, teasing the hard points, before he lowered his head so that he could tease first one, then the other, with his hot mouth and tongue and teeth.

Then his mouth was on hers, swallowing her cry as he seated himself with one smooth thrust, deep inside her. Everything quickened. She was so primed she couldn't hold back a series of shattering orgasms, and she felt Arkim's struggle as he fought to hang on... But it was too much. He pulled free of her clasping body at the last moment and the hot spurt of his seed landed on her belly and breasts. His face was drawn back into a silent scream of ecstasy.

The lash of his essence on her skin felt like a brand, and intensely erotic. But as suddenly as she felt that, Sylvie felt cold, in spite of the heat and languor in her bones. Because she ached with wanting to feel his seed lodged deep inside her, where it might create life, connecting her to this man for ever.

* * *

'Are you planning on dropping off the radar for good?'

Arkim scowled into the satellite phone and answered his executive assistant. 'Of course not.'

'Good, because the deal with Lewis is still on—just about. But you need to be here to deal with it.'

After a few more minutes of discussion Arkim ended the call. He was on a horse, on a sand dune, looking down over the oasis.

He could see Sylvie's bright red hair as she played with a group of the nomad children, chasing them. He could hear their squeals of delight from here. Her skin had taken on a golden glow and more delicate freckles, in spite of the high-factor sun cream he insisted she wear every day.

He felt himself smiling, and a sense of deep contentment was flowing over him and through him. Along with that piquant edge of desire never far from the surface whether Sylvie was in sight or not.

His smile faded when he thought of that first night again. He'd been convinced he'd have to take them both back to civilisation after she'd walked out on him—justifiably—with all the hauteur of a queen. What she'd told him about the legacy of her father had eaten away at his guts like acid: *'When you've protected yourself against rejection your whole life it's almost a relief not to have to fear it any more.'* But ultimately he hadn't been strong enough to walk away. Or to send her away. So he'd been selfish. And taken her for himself.

And even though she'd told him so fiercely, *'You're not your father...'* he was afraid that he was. That he still had some deep flaw inside him. Yet somehow, right now, looking down at that bright head, the assertion didn't sting as much as it usually did.

He'd always ensured his lovers never strayed beyond the firm boundaries he laid down. He always went to their places, or met them in hotels. He never brought them to his personal space. Never encouraged them to talk of personal matters.

And he never spirited them away to a desert oasis to lose himself in their bodies before he went crazy...

'Are you planning on dropping off the radar for good?'

It suddenly struck him: *what the hell was he doing?* His smile faded completely and he went cold inside. His reputation still hung in the balance, and it was thanks to that woman's actions.

He'd meted out his vengeance. He'd had her under him, begging for release. *But not for forgiveness.* At what point had Arkim forgotten that?

Around the first time Sylvie opened her legs to you...

It started hitting him like a series of blows about the head and face. Just how much he'd let her in. Just how much he'd told her. And all because since the moment she'd arrived she'd been nothing like he'd expected. The biggest revelation of all having been her innocence. Her physical innocence.

He had to force himself to acknowledge now that that was as far as her innocence went. She still hadn't told him her reasons for disrupting the wedding that day.

Something trickled down his neck and spine. A sense of having been monumentally naive. Moments ago—before Arkim had had that phone conversation—he'd been contemplating what might happen after Al-Omar. He'd contemplated keeping Sylvie on as his lover. Because he didn't see an end in sight to this ravenous desire. The more he had of her, the more he wanted.

From his vantage point now he could see the children scattering as someone called them, the cry lifted on the wind.

Sylvie stood and looked up to where he was, shaded her eyes. Arkim felt her pull even from here as the breeze moulded the long tunic she wore to her body, showing off the curves of her high, full breasts.

He imagined a scenario of returning to civilisation and allowing Sylvie to slip under his skin even more indelibly. She was the last woman he needed in his life right now—right when everything hung in the balance *because of her.*

With a sharp kick of his heel on his horse's flank he made his way back to the oasis. He knew what he had to do.

'Look! It's a puppy with eyes like mine!'

Sylvie was sitting cross-legged outside Arkim's tent, more happy than she cared to admit to see him returning from his satellite phone call, even if he did look very grim. She held up a squirming bundle of white fur with a tail, yapping intermittently.

Arkim crouched down and Sylvie held it so he could see the puppy's brown and blue eyes. There was something about Arkim's grimness that made her say nervously, 'Sadim, one of the younger boys, showed him to me. They were excited because of the similarity...the eye discolouration.'

He straightened up again. 'You shouldn't be handling it—dogs around here are feral.'

Sylvie's sense of something being wrong increased. Arkim's tone was harsh in a way she hadn't heard in days.

She stood up too, cradling the dog against her chest, feeling at a disadvantage. 'He's not feral... he's gorgeous.'

The small boy Sylvie had spoken of hovered nearby. With a brusque movement Arkim gestured him over. He took the puppy out of Sylvie's arms, his hands brushing against her breasts perfunctorily, and handed it back to the boy, saying something that made the boy look at him as if he'd just kicked the puppy before he ran off.

Sylvie stared at him. 'What did you do that for?'

Arkim was definitely harsh now. 'Because we don't have time for this. It's time to leave...I have to return to London.'

'Oh, is everything okay?' Sylvie struggled to assimilate Arkim's change in mood and this news.

'I've arranged for the helicopter to come for you in a couple of hours. Halima will ensure your bags from the castle are on board.'

'For me?' Sylvie repeated faintly, aware that Arkim hadn't really answered her question.

His face was expressionless, and it made Sylvie think of the passionate intensity he'd shown in bed only a few hours before. It suddenly felt like a long time ago. Not hours.

'Yes, for you,' Arkim reiterated. 'The helicopter will take you to the international airport in B'harani, where one of my staff will meet you and see you on to a plane back to France. I'm taking the Jeep back to the castle as I've some business to attend to there before I return to Europe.'

When she said nothing, feeling cold inside, and as if she'd been hit with a bat, Arkim asked almost accusingly, 'Did you think we could stay here for ever?'

Yes, came a rogue voice. And Sylvie felt like such a fool. She'd been weaving daydreams and fantasies out of something that didn't exist. This oasis and what had happened here was as much of a mirage as the kind a dying man in the desert might see through the heat waves in the distance. For ever unreachable.

She forced herself to look Arkim in the eye. 'No, of course not.'

His voice was stark, stripped of anything remotely soft. 'This can't ever be anything more than what's happened here. You *do* know that, don't you?'

Sylvie felt her old cynical walls—badly battered and crumbled—start to resurrect themselves. What Arkim really meant was, *You didn't really think I'd ever want to be associated with you outside of this remote outpost, did you?*

She couldn't believe she'd let herself fall so hard and so fast for someone who would only ever hold her in mediocre esteem. Who had only seduced her as a form of retribution. And she'd been fully complicit.

'Of course I know that, Arkim.' She tried to inject as much nonchalance into her voice as possible.

She felt brittle. If someone so much as brushed past her now she might shatter. She stepped back—out of the pull Arkim exerted on her with such effortless ease.

'I should pack my things. I don't want there to be any delay when the helicopter gets here.'

'Mariah will bring you some lunch.'

Sylvie forced a smile. 'That's considerate—thank you.'

She turned and walked away before he could see

the rise of tumultuous emotions within her. Anger and hurt and self-recrimination. She should have left when she had the chance. She should have protected herself better. She should have known that he would just drop her from a height when he was done with her... She just hadn't expected it to be so soon, so cold, and so brutal.

A month later, London...

Arkim stood at his office window, gazing out on a scene of unremitting grey skies and rain. An English summer in all its glory.

He realised, somewhat moodily, that he seemed to be spending an inordinate amount of time looking out of his window across the iconic cityscape, with an inability to focus.

Since he'd come back to London he'd been braced for the fallout from his very public humiliation. But, to his shock and surprise, when he'd requested a debriefing from his PR team he'd been informed that there *was* no discernible fallout. Yes, he'd lost some business initially, and the tabloid reports in the immediate aftermath had been bruising. Stocks had fallen sharply, but it had been very temporary. And ultimately not damaging.

Arkim was not a little stunned to realise that in the wake of his ruined wedding, the world hadn't stopped turning. The reputation he'd spent so long building up hadn't crumbled to pieces, as he'd feared. Many more scandals had come and gone. He was already old news. People couldn't care less if he'd really slept with Sylvie Devereux.

The deal with Grant Lewis had been signed off on, and the old man appeared to feel no rancour towards Arkim, despite what had happened. Lewis had been in straits far more dire than he'd led anyone to believe, and his eagerness to keep the deal on the table only reminded Arkim of how eroded his well-worn cynicism had become. Lust for power and wealth trumped even scandal.

A hum of ever-present frustration pulsed in his blood. Despite his best efforts to resist the urge, he'd had his team checking the papers and media daily for any news of Sylvie, but to all intents and purposes she'd vanished back into her life.

An image of her face, wide open and smiling, her skin lightly golden from the sun and dusted with freckles, came back to him so vividly that he sucked in a breath.

An ache had settled deep into his being from the moment he'd watched her helicopter take off from the oasis that day and it hadn't subsided. The truth could no longer be ignored or denied. *He still wanted her.*

In the last month he'd been to functions with the most beautiful women in the world, and they'd left him cold. Dead inside. But all he had to do was conjure up a memory of Sylvie—*that day in the pool*—and he was rewarded with a surge of arousal. About which he could do nothing unless he wanted to regress to being the age of fourteen in a shower stall.

The intercom sounded from his desk and Arkim welcomed the distraction, turning around. 'Yes, Liz?'

'There's a young lady downstairs to see you...'

Even before Arkim could ask her name, blood was rushing to his head and heat to his groin.

'Who did you say?' He had to ask, after his assistant had said the name. Surely he'd misheard—?

'Sophie Lewis...your...er...ex-fiancée.'

Disappointment was acute. So acute that Arkim knew he had a problem. And what on earth could Sophie Lewis possibly want with the man who had—allegedly—been unfaithful to her with her own sister?

'Send her up,' he said grimly.

* * *

Sylvie had finished rehearsals with Pierre and the rest of the revue for the day and had stayed behind at the dance studios to practise on her own for her modern dance class.

She focused on the music and the athletic movements of her body, clad in dance leggings and a cropped tank top. Her hair was up in a high ponytail and her skin was sheened with perspiration from the exertion. But the burn of her muscles and the intense focus was good. Anything to block *him* and the fact that she would never see him again out of her mind. Block out the fact that he wanted nothing to do with her. That what had happened meant nothing to him…

Sylvie made an awkward move and landed heavily on her foot. Damn. *Damn him for invading her thoughts.*

She bent down over her foot, but thankfully she hadn't strained it. They were close to the opening night for the relaunch of the club—Pierre would never forgive her if she injured herself now…especially when she wasn't even practising the revue's routines.

She stood up straight in front of the long mirror that spanned one whole wall and stretched her neck. She was about to start at the beginning again when she saw something move, and she looked towards where the door was reflected in the mirror to see a big dark shape.

Arkim.

This was really getting to be too much. Now she was seeing things. She blinked. But he didn't go away.

The door was pushed open and he walked in. Dressed in dark trousers and a light shirt, sleeves rolled up, top button open. As if he'd just strolled in from a nearby office.

Slowly, eyes widening, Sylvie turned around, half expecting him not to be there when she faced him. But he was. He was real.

To her utter horror she felt a welling of emotion: a mixture of anger, relief and the sheer need to run to him and wrap herself so tightly around him he wouldn't be able to breathe.

She took a deep, steadying breath, and curled her hands into fists. Had she already forgotten the brutality with which he'd let her go that day at the oasis? Coldly. Summarily.

Praying her voice wouldn't betray her, and lamenting her less than pristine physical state, she said coolly, 'Hello, Arkim.'

'Hello, Sylvie.'

That voice. *His* voice. It reached inside her and squeezed tight. She remembered him saying *Sylvie* with a guttural groan as his climax had made his whole body go taut over hers.

'I can't imagine that you were just passing.'

Arkim put his hands in his pockets and walked into the room, his every step gracefully athletic. Masculine. He was clean-shaven. And he'd had a haircut.

He was still quite simply the most astoundingly handsome man she'd ever seen.

He stopped a couple of feet away. Close enough for his scent to tickle her nostrils and for her body to go into meltdown at his proximity. Her heart seemed to have been in shock, because it started again at about triple its normal rate.

'No, I wasn't just passing. I came especially. To see you.'

She dampened down the surge of excitement. Her hurt at the way he'd sent her off was still acute. She lifted her chin. 'Why? Did I leave something behind?'

Arkim's face was impassive, but she saw a muscle work in his jaw. His throat moved. Sylvie could have spent hours just studying every minute part of his olive-skinned anatomy. *She had.*

'You could say that. *Me.*'

Her eyes clashed with the darkest brown. Incredulity made her mouth gape before she found the wherewithal to say, 'I left *you* behind?'

'Yes...' he breathed, and moved even closer.

His eyes were roving hungrily over her now, making a hot flush spread out all over Sylvie's body from between her legs. This man had changed her utterly, in so many ways. So much so that the minute Pierre had seen her again the older patriarchal man had looked her up and down and said accusingly, 'Something's different...what's happened to you?'

Sylvie had been mortified beyond belief to think that someone might be able to *see* what had happened to her. But she could feel it even when she danced. A new awareness of her body...her sexuality.

She crossed her arms over her chest and glared at Arkim, the architect of all of this. His eyes met hers again and she saw the fire in them. But before she could say anything—not even sure what she *wanted* to say—he asked, 'What was that dancing you were just doing? It was different to the way you danced for me.'

Taken aback, Sylvie said, 'It's something I'm working on for my contemporary dance class.'

'I liked it…it was beautiful.'

And just like that Sylvie's jagged emotions stopped pricking her. 'You did?'

Arkim reached out and touched a loose tendril of hair. He nodded. 'You looked as if you were lost in another world.'

She was finding it hard to breathe. 'I choreographed the dance.'

It was only when she said it that she felt totally exposed. A lot of that dance had been born out of the pain she'd felt for the past month.

She stepped back and his hand fell away. His eyes flashed. Still the same arrogant Arkim. And what had he meant when he'd said she'd left him behind?

'What do you want, Arkim? I haven't finished practising, and I only have this space for another twenty minutes.'

'I want to talk to you. And I have something for you at my apartment.'

'Your apartment?'

'I have an apartment here in Paris. I'm working here for the next few weeks—in my Paris office.'

Of *course* he had an office and an apartment here. He *would*.

But still, she resisted. 'Why, Arkim? Why do we have to talk? I think we said everything, don't you? Or you certainly did, anyway.'

He looked for a moment, as if he didn't want to say anything, but then he did. 'Your sister came to see me...I *know*, Sylvie.'

Sylvie could feel her blood draining south so quickly that she swayed. Immediately Arkim's hand was on her arm. To her awful shame, her first thought was not of Sophie but of the fact that Arkim hadn't come because he wanted her back at all...

'Sophie...came to see you?' Sylvie was vaguely aware that her phone had been off all day during rehearsals, so she'd been uncontactable.

He nodded. Grim. 'Look, finish your practice. I'll wait, and then you'll come with me...yes?'

There was no way Sylvie could focus now. She'd break her ankle. And that was just at the thought of Arkim waiting for her. She shook her head. 'No, I'll change now and come with you.'

She had no choice. She had to know what Sophie's visit to him meant. And that was *all* Arkim wanted to talk to her about. As long as she remembered that she'd be okay.

He let her go. 'I'll wait for you downstairs. My car is at the door.'

As Arkim waited in the back of his chauffeur-driven car he couldn't dampen down the swell of triumph...or the swell of his erection. His whole body had gone on fire as soon as he'd seen Sylvie through the door...her lithe dancer's body moving with such grace and power...in a way he'd never seen before. Beautiful, elegant...passionate. He'd been mesmerised. In awe. In lust.

She'd looked wary at seeing him again, even though he'd felt the resurgence of the powerful sexual connection between them. Yet could he blame her for being wary? He'd behaved like an idiot that last day at the oasis... He'd been acting on a knee-jerk reflex to get rid of Sylvie before she slid herself even more indelibly under his skin... but it had been too late.

He had to concede that even if Sophie hadn't come—

His thoughts stopped working as Sylvie walked out through the door, her vibrant hair tied back in a knot—damp from a shower? She wore faded skinny jeans that showed her long legs off to perfection, ballet flats and a loose off-the-shoulder T-shirt, with the straps of a vest visible underneath. Her skin was pale again...like a pearl.

Arkim let his driver get out to open the door for her. He literally couldn't move for fear of making a complete idiot of himself.

When she slid into the back seat on the other side she didn't look at him, putting her slouchy bag firmly on her lap as she strapped her seat belt on. Arkim wanted to reach across and force her to meet his eyes, force her to know how much he wanted her before he crushed that soft mouth under his and found some sense of peace for the first time in a month.

A flutter of panic at the strength of how much he wanted her made his gut tighten. How relieved he'd been as soon as he'd laid eyes on her...

Sylvie Devereux was still completely wrong for him on so many levels. This was lust. Pure and simple. Unprecedented, but not without its sell-by date.

Then she looked at him with those wide eyes, blue and blue-green, and Arkim's thoughts scattered to pieces.

'Why did Sophie come to see you?'

Arkim dragged his brain back into some kind of functioning order. 'She told me everything.'

CHAPTER NINE

THE CAR WAS moving at a snail's pace in the early-evening Paris traffic as Arkim's words sank in. And even though Sylvie was preoccupied by what he was saying, and what it meant, she was acutely aware of that big, powerful body so close to hers. Legs spread, chest broad.

She had to get it together. *Sophie.* Hesitantly she asked, 'When you say "everything", do you mean—?'

'I mean,' Arkim said, cutting her off, 'I know that she's gay, Sylvie. She told me everything. About how she was afraid to come out. About how she was railroaded into marriage by her parents because they thought it would sweeten the deal for me. I'd made no attempt to hide the fact that I wanted to settle in England, and I wasn't averse to settling down with a suitable wife.'

The kind of wife who would remove Arkim permanently from his sordid past... Sylvie thought to herself, with a lurch of pain near her heart.

He continued, 'She told me about her girlfriend in college, and how she was too terrified to stand up to her mother…that she's always had trouble standing up to her.' Arkim's mouth twisted. 'I can understand why.'

Sylvie reeled. 'My God…she really *did* tell you everything.'

Arkim nodded. 'She also told me that she'd refused to let you do anything at first, because she didn't want you to damage your already contentious relationship with your father and stepmother, and they'd inevitably blame you even though it had nothing to do with you… But the week of the wedding she was panicking so much that she accepted your offer to step in at the last minute if she needed it. Which is what you did…in your own inimitable way.'

Sylvie blushed, thinking of that daring moment again. Arkim looked equable enough right now, but she knew how deep his emotions went, and how he simmered.

Trepidation gripped her. 'Were you angry with her?'

For a second he just looked at her, and then he said with faint incredulity, 'Even now your first concern is whether or not I got angry with her?'

Sylvie squirmed. 'Well, I know how intimidating you can be.'

Arkim's mouth thinned. 'At first I was angry, yes.' He reacted to the look that crossed Sylvie's face. 'I had a right to be. Both of you made me a laughing stock. If Sophie had just come to me and explained I would have understood. I'm not such an ogre. *Hell*.'

He turned away in disgust, to look out of the window. Sylvie felt immediately chastened. She knew that he wouldn't have taken it out on Sophie...all of Arkim's anger was only ever for *her*.

She pushed down the sense of futility. 'You're right,' she said in a quiet voice. 'I should have come to you myself and said something... If we'd been able to stop the wedding a week before it would have avoided the messy scandal it became. But I knew how unlikely it was that you'd believe anything I said...'

Some of the tension seemed to leave his shoulders. He turned back, those black eyes like pools of obsidian. To Sylvie's surprise, his mouth quirked ever so slightly on one side.

'I guess I have to give you that...I would have seen it as just another jealous attempt to make me notice you.' His expression became shuttered. 'I believed you were *jealous*...you let me believe that, like a fool.'

She knew she owed him total honesty now—especially after Sophie's bravery—albeit belated. She forced herself to look at him. 'The truth is... as much as I was doing it for Sophie I *was* jealous. I wanted you...for myself.'

She hadn't even properly admitted that to herself until this moment. Her head felt light.

Arkim's eyes gleamed. He breathed out. 'I *knew* it...'

For a second she thought he was about to reach for her, and her whole body tingled, but then a discreet tap came from nearby. It took a minute for her to figure out that the driver was knocking on the partition, alerting them to the fact that they'd pulled up outside a building on a quiet street.

Sylvie felt a little dizzy. She looked out of the window and didn't immediately recognise much, except for the fact that they were in a very expensive part of Paris. Her voice was husky. 'Where are we?'

'My apartment building on the Île Saint-Louis.'

She looked back to Arkim. She felt confused, she wasn't sure where they stood any more.

He said, 'I have something for you upstairs.'

She joked weakly, 'That's not a very original chat-up line.'

He was serious. 'It's not a chat-up line. I really *do* have something for you.'

'Oh.' She instantly felt silly. The driver—as if knowing just the perfect moment to capitalise on her doubts—appeared at her door and opened it. By the time she was standing, clutching her bag, Arkim was waiting for her, darkly handsome and very vital-looking against the grey stone of the old building.

How was it that he could look so devastating, no matter what milieu he was in? she grumbled to herself as she let him lead her into the building. She felt very dishevelled when she saw the marble floor and discreetly exquisite furnishings. And the uniformed concierge who treated Arkim like royalty.

There was a lift attendant, and Sylvie almost felt like giggling. It was so far removed from the constantly out of use elevator in her rickety building in Montmartre.

The lift came to a smooth stop and Arkim led her into a luxuriously carpeted hall, with one door at the end. He opened it and she walked in cautiously, her eyes widening as she took in the parquet floors and quietly sumptuous decor.

The reception rooms were spacious, with floor-to-ceiling French doors looking out over Paris and the Seine. The furniture was antique, but not fussy. Comfortable, inviting.

Drawn by something she'd spotted, she walked over to the opposite side of the room and stood before a black and white photo.

'It's Al-Hibiz.'

Arkim's voice was close enough to set Sylvie's nerve endings alight. 'Yes,' she said, remembering her first view of the majestic castle. A terrible sense of longing for that wide open landscape washed over her. *The oasis.*

This was torture, being so close to Arkim again and yet not really knowing what he wanted from her. She whirled around and he was a lot closer than she'd expected, within touching distance.

'Arkim?' Her voice croaked humiliatingly.

He was staring at her mouth. 'Yes...'

So she looked at his...at the strong sensual lines. And his jaw, so resolute. From the moment she'd first seen him she'd had that instinct to smooth the stark lines of his face.

She didn't know who moved first, but it was

as if attracting ions finally overcame the tension between them, and then she was in his arms, her whole body straining against his, her arms tight around his neck. Their mouths were fused, tongues tangled in a desperate hungry kiss, the breath being sucked out of each other's bodies to mix and mingle and go on fire. Arkim's hands shaped and cupped Sylvie's buttocks, lifting her up, encouraging her legs to wrap around him.

She wasn't even aware that Arkim had collapsed onto a couch behind them until she pulled back from the kiss to gasp in air and realised that her thighs were wedged open, tight against his, and she could feel the potent thrust of his arousal against where she ached.

She felt shaky. The fire had blasted up around them so quickly. 'Arkim...what are we—?'

He put a finger to her lips. He looked fierce. 'Don't say anything—please. I need this. I need *you*. Now.'

There was something raw in his tone...something that resonated deep inside her. Who was she kidding? She needed this too. Desperately.

She levered herself against him, pushing back. Infused with a sense of confidence borne out of what this man had given her at that oasis, Sylvie stood up and slowly and methodically took off her clothes until she was naked.

He looked...stunned. Hypnotised. In shock. In awe.

Sylvie came back and straddled him again, every inch of her skin sensitised just from his look. His hands came to her waist and she felt a slight tremor in them. She reached down between them and undid his trousers, pulled him free, smoothing her hand up and down the silken length of his erection, her whole body flushing red with lust.

The fact that she was naked and he was still almost fully dressed was erotic in the extreme. But when Arkim's mouth latched on to her nipple, Sylvie's fleeting sense of being in control quickly evaporated, and he skilfully showed her who was the real master here. She was rubbing against him, thick and hard between her legs, feeling her juices anointing his shaft.

Arkim groaned and dropped his head against her and said, 'I need to be inside you...*now*.'

Sylvie raised herself up in wordless acquiescence while Arkim extricated protection from his pocket, smoothing the thin latex sheath onto his penis.

His hands were back on her waist—tight, urgent. He positioned her so that her slick body rested just over his tip and with exquisite care, as if savouring the moment, he brought Sylvie down onto his erection. She inhaled as he filled her, almost to the point of pain but still on the side of pleasure. When he was as deep as he could go he held her there for a moment, before it got too much and he had to move again...

There was nothing but the sound of their laboured breathing in the quiet apartment as the frenzy overtook them. Her knees were pressed to his thighs, her hands gripping his shoulders. Her whole body tightened and quickened as Arkim thrust hard and deep up into her, hips welded to hers. He was so deep...deeper than ever before. She could feel her heart beating out of time. And when the explosion hit there was nowhere to hide.

Sylvie's head was thrown back, her eyes shut, every muscle and sinew taut, as waves and waves of release flowed through her body, wrenching her soul apart. And Arkim was with her every step of the way, his own body as taut as a whip under hers.

It was so excruciatingly exquisite that it almost

felt like a punishment. As if Arkim was doing this on purpose, just to torture her. It was shattering.

And when the waves subsided Sylvie subsided too, unable to keep herself upright, collapsing against Arkim's chest, her head buried in his neck.

She felt like a car crash victim. As if some kind of explosion had really just happened, knocking her out of orbit. The fact that his heart was thundering under hers was no consolation. Her skin was hot, sticky, but she was too wiped out to care.

She whispered into his damp neck, 'What are we doing?'

She felt Arkim's chest swell underneath hers, making her sensitive breasts ache. His voice rumbled around her.

'We're doing that again...as soon as I can move...'

Much later, when it was dark outside, Sylvie woke alone in a massive bed. She was disorientated for a moment, and then the pleasurable aches and tingles in her body and the tenderness between her legs helped her to remember the last few cataclysmic hours.

Arkim had been true to his word. As soon as he'd been able to move he'd carried Sylvie into the bedroom, stripped, and proceeded to make love to her all over again. Then they'd taken a shower... and barely made it back to the bed before making love again.

Sylvie groaned and rolled over, mashing her face into a soft pillow. What was she *doing*?

She flipped back again and looked up at the exquisitely corniced ceiling, her mind racing with the implications of what it all meant. Arkim knew now. He knew everything. Everything she hadn't been able to tell him out of loyalty to her sister.

Feeling curious, and wondering where he was, Sylvie sat up, wincing as tender muscles protested. She saw a robe at the end of the bed and reached for it, sitting up to pull it on. It dwarfed her slim frame but she belted it tightly around her, blushing when she thought of her clothes, which must still be strewn in that elegant reception room.

She padded barefoot out of the bedroom and back towards the main part of the apartment. As she was passing a door that was slightly ajar she noticed a dim golden light and heard a suspicious-sounding *yap*.

She pushed open the door to find a study, three walls lined with bookshelves and books. A huge desk was in front of the window, its surface covered with a computer, laptop and papers… But her eyes nearly popped out of her head when she saw Arkim sitting on the ground, his back against the only bare wall in the room, wearing only a pair of sweats and cradling a familiar-looking puppy in his arms.

They both looked up at the same time, and it would have been comical if Sylvie hadn't been so shocked. The little dog shot out of Arkim's arms and raced over to Sylvie, yapping excitedly, its stubby little tail waggling furiously. She crouched down and was almost bowled over by his enthusiasm, his tongue licking wherever he could reach.

When she was over her shock she looked at Arkim, who was still sitting there, looking for all the world as if nothing untoward was going on. 'What on earth…? How did you get him here?'

And why? Sylvie wanted to ask, but was afraid.

Arkim shrugged one shoulder negligently. 'I brought him back to the castle with me that day… and then I just ended up bringing him to Europe.'

Sylvie's breath felt choppy all of a sudden, and her heart was thumping hard. In a flight of fancy in her head she was imagining all sorts of reasons that were all very, *very* dangerous.

She buried her nose in his fur. When she looked up again she said, 'He's all cleaned up...what is he?'

Arkim's mouth quirked. 'A Highland Westie mixed with something indeterminate.'

'Have you got a name for him yet?'

He shook his head. 'I couldn't think of one. But I want to give him to you...so you choose a name.'

Sylvie's mouth fell open and the dog squirmed to be free, so she let him out of her arms to go sniffing at something exciting nearby. 'But...but I can't take him. My apartment is tiny, and Giselle is allergic to animal hair.'

Arkim frowned. 'Giselle?'

Sylvie waved a hand. 'My flatmate. Arkim... why are you doing this?'

He rose lithely from his seat on the floor, his chest dark under its smattering of hair in the golden light. He came over to her and held out a hand. Sylvie took it and he pulled her up. He led her over to a seat and sat down, pulling her into his lap. He smoothed her trailing hair over one shoulder.

She felt extremely unsure of her footing, and vulnerable. 'Arkim—'

'That day...' he interjected.

She nodded.

'I regretted sending you away like that.'

Sylvie's heart palpitations were back. 'You did?'

He nodded, his black eyes on hers, not letting her look away. 'I was a coward. You were getting too close...I asked you if you'd thought we were going to stay there for ever, but the truth is I think that's exactly what *I* wanted. Never to leave. And it just hit me: I had a life to get back to and I'd almost forgotten it existed. That *I* existed outside of that place. I honestly haven't been able to stop thinking about you. We're not done, Sylvie...I need more time with you.'

'What exactly are you saying, Arkim?' Sylvie didn't like the unpalatable questions being thrown up by his choice of words. *'I need more time with you...'* It sounded finite. Definitely finite.

'I want you to move in with me. Stay with me for as long as...'

'For as long as what?' she asked sharply, tensing all over. Because she very badly wanted him to say, *For as long as you want. For ever.*

'For as long as this lasts...this crazy, insatiable desire.'

Finite. Definitely finite.

She pulled away from Arkim and stood up before he could see how raw she felt. The puppy sniffed around her feet and she picked him up and held him against her, almost like a shield. How could Arkim manipulate her like this? Give her a reminder of the exquisite pleasure he could wring from her body...tell her he regretted the way he'd behaved...the puppy...and now this. When her defences were down.

Because this is the man who all but kidnapped you and held you in his castle at his pleasure when he wanted revenge.

She pushed aside the memories crowding her head. She needed to lay it out baldly for herself. 'So you're asking me to become your mistress? Is that it? And the dog is meant to sweeten the deal?' She made a sound of disgust and turned round to face the window. How could she have been so stupid...so—?

She was whirled around again to face Arkim, looming tall and intimidating.

'*No*...it's not like that. I mean...yes, I want you to stay—but as my lover...not as a mistress.' He sounded almost bitter. 'Believe me, I know by now that you would never languish idly at someone's beck and call. And the dog... I hadn't even consciously realised I wanted him for you, but I got your address from Sophie and I brought him with me. I don't take mistresses,' he said. 'I thought you'd know me well enough by now to know that I don't indulge women like that. I don't do frills or niceties.'

No. He didn't. He could tear a woman's heart and soul to shreds just by being him. Raw. Male. Uncompromising. Tortured, but with a deep core of emotion that made her heart break.

'You were right, you know,' he said heavily.

Sylvie finally found her voice. 'About what?'

Arkim grimaced. 'About my motivations for agreeing to marry Sophie. She represented something to me—something I'd always craved. A respectable family unit.'

And that just confirmed for Sylvie what she'd already guessed. Some day Arkim would find a woman worthy of being his perfectly respectable wife, and then he *would* do frills and niceties. She didn't doubt it.

The hatred she felt for that future woman shocked her. But it also made her see her own weakness. She wanted more too. She wanted to take every atom of what Arkim was offering and gorge herself before he cast her aside again. Or— if she had the strength—gorge herself so that she could walk away before he could do it for her.

She lifted her chin. 'If I stay with you and we... we do this, I won't give up my job.'

Arkim was very still. 'I wouldn't expect you to.'

Sylvie felt a spurt of relief mixed with pain. As long as she stayed in her 'job of ill repute' she'd remember who she was—and so would he. There would be no dangerous illusions or dreams, no fantasies that things could be different. Because they never could be. She was *not* the woman who would share Arkim's life and mother his children. And she needed to remember that.

She forced a lightness to her voice that she wasn't feeling and said, 'Well, then, if this dog is really mine I'd better think of a name.'

'That's a *good* boy, Omar...'

Arkim stood at the door and watched Sylvie hand the puppy a treat from her pocket as she lavished him with praise, rubbing him behind his floppy ears. As far as he could tell the dog wasn't doing anything that vaguely resembled obeying commands, but Sylvie was too besotted to care.

He recalled the spontaneous urge he'd felt to take the dog with him when he'd been leaving the oasis, obeying some irrational impulse because it had been the last thing Sylvie had touched. And then he'd spent a month tripping over the damn thing in London, talking to it as if it could understand him.

An alien lightness vied with a familiar surge of arousal just to see her sitting on the floor, her hair in a plait down her back. She was obviously just back from work, still dressed in leggings and a loose top. Arkim was used to women in couture creations and the latest ready-to-wear casuals. Yet Sylvie would blow them all out of the water with her inherent grace and elegance, dressed just like this.

She insisted on taking the Métro every day, refusing his offer of a driver and car. And he hadn't even realised that his kitchen functioned until he'd come in one evening and found Sylvie taking a Boeuf Bourguignon out of the oven. Far from making him break out in a cold sweat at the domesticity, he'd found it surprisingly appealing. He'd never known what it was to come home to a cooked meal, and he'd found himself laughing out loud at Sylvie's wry tales of learning to cook when she'd first arrived in Paris.

When she'd told him that she regularly baked for the members of the revue, he'd found his conscience smarting at the thought of how badly he'd misjudged her from that first moment he'd laid eyes on her. Because at first glance she'd epitomised everything he'd grown up to despise in a lewd, over-sexualised world.

In fact she was anything but. He'd been wrong about her. *So* wrong.

It had been two weeks now since she'd moved in...and just like before, the more Arkim had of her, the more he wanted her. It made him nervous. This...this lust he felt was too urgent. Desperate, even. He couldn't let her go. *Yet.*

She looked up then and saw him standing there. Her eyes widened, brightened, and she smiled. But then the smile slipped slightly and a guarded look came over her beautiful face. It made Arkim want to haul her up and demand that she... *What?* asked a small voice. *Stop shutting you out?*

Ever since that night when she'd agreed to stay Sylvie had locked a piece of herself away from him. She was careful around him—there was some spark he'd come to expect in her missing.

Except for when they made love... Then she could hold nothing back, in spite of herself.

But when they were finished she would curl up on her side, away from him. And Arkim would lie there and clench his hands into fists to stop himself from reaching for her—because he didn't do that, did he? That would send the wrong message...that this was something more than a transitory slaking of mutual lust.

Except it wasn't being slaked. It was being stoked.

'A function?' Sylvie felt a flicker of trepidation. So far she and Arkim had spent their time confined to his stunning apartment. They met here after work and indulged in satisfying their mutual lust until they couldn't move. Then they got up, went to work and repeated the process.

Every morning Sylvie woke up praying that this would be the morning when he didn't affect her so much...to no avail. And when they'd had dinner the other night...dinner she'd made...it had felt far too easy...seductive. She couldn't do that again.

Arkim was leaning against the doorframe, looking edible in a dark three-piece suit, his jaw stubbled after the day.

'It's a charity benefit thing...to raise money for cancer awareness. I thought you'd have an interest.'

Sylvie was shocked that Arkim obviously remembered her telling him that her mother had died of cancer.

'Well, of course I do… But…I mean, I didn't think you'd want to be seen with me. In public.'

Some fleeting expression passed over his face and then he came over and pulled her up from the floor, his hands resting under her arms. 'The reason we haven't gone out together is because the minute I see you I need you. And I need you now.'

Everything in Sylvie exulted. She felt exactly the same. The insatiable desire to cleave herself to this man.

She was barely aware of Omar—she'd named him after Al-Omar—pawing her calf, looking for attention.

'What about the function?' The thought of going out in public with Arkim was alternately terrifying and exciting.

'We're still going… But first…a shower?'

Sylvie hid her reaction to the fact that he was prepared to be seen in public with her and said, mock seriously, 'I think your dedication to water conservation is to be commended.'

Arkim snorted and tugged her to the bedroom, shutting the door firmly on Omar, who skidded to a stop outside the closed door and proceeded to whine pitifully and unnoticed for the next half an hour.

'Are you sure I look okay?'

Arkim was the epitome of civilised style in a black tuxedo. Sylvie hated feeling so insecure, but the full magnitude of what this public outing meant was sinking in—and not in a good way. She was nervous of people recognising him, recognising *her*, and the inevitable scrutiny.

He reached for her hand, lacing his fingers through hers. 'You look amazing. Just think of this as one of your father's events…you looked pretty confident to me in that milieu.'

She fought back a blush to think of how forward she'd been and plucked at the silky emerald-green material of her dress. The dress was gorgeous—a slinky column of pure silk—it covered her from throat to wrist to ankle but, perversely, it felt more revealing than anything she'd ever worn before, skimming close to her curves and cut on the bias.

It had been waiting for her in a silver embossed box when she'd emerged from her shower with Arkim, barely able to walk after his *very* careful ministrations. Every feminist principle in her had risen up to refuse it…but she'd taken one look and fallen in love. It reminded her poignantly of a dress her mother had owned—which Catherine had inevitably thrown out—and so, like a traitor, she'd accepted it.

She'd styled her hair into movie star waves and hoped that it wasn't too much. She knew how snobbish these events were, and if anyone recognised her… She gulped.

'Relax…I know how you feel—believe me.'

Sylvie was jolted out of her introspection and she looked at the wry expression on Arkim's face. Of course he knew. He was the son of one of the most infamous men in the world. When she thought of how proud he was… Her heart felt ominously achy at the thought of people looking at him and judging him.

As he did you, she reminded herself. And even though she could understand his motives now the hurt still lingered.

The car was drawing to a smooth stop outside one of Paris's most iconic and glamorous hotels. Arkim got out, and Sylvie drew in a deep breath as he opened the door and held out a hand for her. They joined a very glitzy throng of beautiful people entering the foyer with lots of expensive perfume and air-kissing. Arkim held Sylvie's hand, and she found she was clinging to him.

She reminded herself that she needed to be vigilant around him. She didn't want to lose herself again so easily. So she forced herself to relax and took her hand out of his, ignoring his look as she squared her shoulders and entered the massive ballroom where the function was being held.

His hand stayed on the small of her back, though, as waiters offered them drinks and they navigated their way around the room, constantly stopping when Arkim was recognised by various people.

Sylvie found, much to her relief, that she was usually given a quick once-over and then summarily dismissed. She didn't mind. She preferred that to scrutiny or recognition any day of the week.

When they were momentarily alone again Sylvie asked curiously, 'When do they announce dinner?' She was beginning to feel hunger pangs after their earlier activity.

Arkim grimaced slightly and gestured with his head to where a waiter was passing, with some teeny-tiny hors d'oeuvres that looked more like art installations than food. 'That's dinner, I'm afraid,

I think most people here haven't eaten in about ten years.'

Sylvie grinned at his humour—and then her stomach growled in earnest and she blushed, ducking her head with embarrassment.

Arkim slid an arm around her waist and pulled her into his tall, hard body, creating a wave of heat that slowly engulfed her. When she looked at him again he said, 'Isn't there some leftover Boeuf Bourguignon at home?'

His use of the word *home* caused butterflies. She fought to stay cool. 'I believe there is...'

Arkim's gaze moved down to her mouth and now *he* looked hungry. 'Then let's get out of here. I've had enough.'

The thought of leaving now, getting out of the evening intact, without any awkward public meetings, was very appealing. Apart from what the explicit hunger in his eyes promised... Well, she *had* made a promise to herself to gorge, hadn't she?

Sylvie looked up at him and felt as if she was drowning. As if she was fighting a losing battle. 'Okay, then—let's go.'

They were walking out through the vast marbled lobby—hand in hand because Arkim refused to let her tug free—and Sylvie was floating on a cloud of dangerous contentment at the thought of being alone with him again, when a group of men stopped in front of them. Arkim stopped, making her jerk to a halt beside him.

She looked up, expecting it to be someone he knew. But the men were looking at *her*. At her body. At her breasts. Before Sylvie had even assessed the situation properly, icy-cold humiliation was crawling up her spine.

'Well, well, well…it's your favourite L'Amour revue artist, James.'

CHAPTER TEN

SYLVIE RECOGNISED THEM—sickeningly. They were regulars at the show—English ex-pats, working in Paris—and one of them had had a brief fling with Giselle, her flatmate. She remembered the guy blearily hopping around their tiny apartment the morning after, looking for his clothes.

Arkim snarled from beside her, 'She doesn't know who you are—now, get out of our way.'

Now all the men's attention was on Arkim. Sylvie wanted to curl up and die. He looked livid. A muscle throbbed in his jaw.

'And who are *you*, mate? Are you paying her well for the night? Cos if you've lost interest we'd be more than happy to stump up some cash for a good time.'

One of the others interjected then. 'She doesn't put out, remember?'

Sylvie felt as if she was in some kind of nightmare. She tried to speak. 'I'm sorry...I really don't think we've met...' But her voice came out all thready and weak, and now the tallest of the men—still a good few inches shorter than Arkim—was standing toe to toe with him.

'Think you're some hotshot, eh? Well, it happens that I recognise you too—*you're* the guy that got stood up at the altar.'

'Oh, God!' Sylvie hadn't even realised she'd spoken out loud. She felt nauseous.

Arkim let her hand go and pushed her away from him, saying in a voice edged with steel, 'Get into the car and wait for me—*now.*'

Sylvie started to back away, horror filling her at the murderous look on Arkim's face, but as she turned around one of the men who so far hadn't said anything blocked her.

'And where do you think *you're* going?'

Sylvie clenched her jaw. 'Get out of my way.'

He came closer and she could smell the reek of alcohol on his breath. 'Now, now…that's not nice, is it? I've *seen* you, you know…'

He stroked a finger up her arm and Sylvie fought not to flinch in disgust.

'You're my favourite of them all…but I'd like to see a lot more of you…'

Sylvie had just positioned her knee for maximum damage, in case he touched her again, and heard an almighty *crack* behind her. She whirled round to see Arkim staggering back, holding a hand up to his eye.

She flew to his side just as the hotel security officers rushed forward. Arkim, still holding a hand to his face, spoke to someone who looked like a manager. The eight or so English guys were rounded up within seconds, and it was only then that Sylvie realised just how drunk they all were, as they were led away with belligerent faces.

Her hand was in Arkim's again, and he was taking her out to the car so fast she had to trot to keep up, holding her dress up. Her stomach was churning painfully, and she breathed out as the car pulled away from the front of the hotel.

She looked at Arkim and winced when she saw his eye, shut tight. She knelt on the seat beside him, swatting aside his hand when he tried to stop her. 'What happened? How did you get hit?'

He looked at her with his one good eye. 'I recognised one of the men.'

Sylvie felt shaky. She reached for a bottle of water and unscrewed it, lifting some of the material at the bottom of her dress and wetting it to dab at his eye ineffectually.

'And?' she prompted, feeling sick all over again.

'He said something about you that I know isn't true.'

Her insides cramped.

'I told him that if he didn't take it back I'd spread the word about his out-of-control recreational drug use. So he hit me.'

Sylvie sat back on her heels, anguished. 'I'm so sorry, Arkim.'

His one good eye glared at her. 'What are you apologising for? *They* were at fault.'

'Yes, but if they hadn't recognised me...'

Arkim didn't say anything, and his silence spoke volumes.

With relief Sylvie saw that they were drawing close to the apartment. The traffic at this time of evening was light, and Arkim didn't live far away. The car pulled to a stop and Arkim got out, his movements jerky. Sylvie didn't wait. She clambered out, still holding her dress up in one hand. The feeling of contentment she'd had earlier had been well and truly shattered by a rude awakening.

In the apartment she could hear Arkim moving restlessly around the drawing room, the clatter of the drinks tray. He was angry. She wrapped some ice in a towel and brought it in, saying as authoritatively as she could, 'Sit down—let me look at you.'

He scowled at her. His jacket was off, his bow tie undone. His eye was closed and swelling. He looked thoroughly disreputable, and it only added to his appeal.

He sat down, legs spread, stretching an arm across the back of the couch. Approaching him, Sylvie felt as if she was approaching a bad-tempered lion. But she did it, and then observed, 'Your eye isn't bleeding—that's good.'

'You're a nurse now?'

Sylvie pushed down a flare of irritation at Arkim's snappy mood. 'No, but I do tend to be the one people come to with minor injuries at work.'

Arkim made a *harumph* sound. Of *course* everyone went to her for treatment at work. He could just imagine her: compassionate, kind, soothing. Yet another unwelcome reminder of how badly he'd misjudged her all along.

He knew he was being a boor, but his gut was still too churned up after the confrontation for him to be sanguine. Sylvie pressed the ice near his eye, and he was aware of her wincing when he sucked in a pained breath.

The words that man had said came back to him: *'She tastes as sweet as she looks, doesn't she?'*

Arkim had had to call on a level of control he'd never used before. And what scared him even now was the instant volcanic jealousy that had swamped him. The tiniest implication that the man had been intimate with Sylvie had been enough to send him into orbit.

He still felt edgy, volatile. Sylvie was kneeling on the couch beside him, the silk of her dress straining across her breasts, outlining their luscious shape. Adrenalin still lingered in Arkim's blood. He needed to channel it…dilute it somehow. Sylvie shifted and her body swayed closer. His arousal spiked, mixing with the adrenalin, making him crave an antidote to this churning in his gut.

He put down his glass of alcohol and reached out and put his hands around Sylvie's waist. She took the ice away and looked at him. Her hair was tumbling over her shoulders, a glossy wave of bright red. She looked concerned. Eyes huge with worry. Remorse.

'Arkim—'

He took the ice pack out of her hands and threw

it aside, then pulled her into him, his intent unmistakable.

Sylvie protested, even though he could feel her breath coming faster, moving her chest against his. 'You're hurt. We can't—'

He put a finger on her mouth, then cupped the back of her head. In spite of his need to devour, consume, he found that something happened as he touched her mouth with his. The tension in his body was fading away…and he was touching her as reverently as if she was made of china.

She braced herself with her hands on his chest. Desire rose up, fast and urgent, replacing the need to be reverent, and Arkim fumbled clumsily with his clothes and body, sheathing himself with protection. Sylvie rose above him, pulling her dress up, eyes glazed with lust, cheeks flushed.

Arkim tore Sylvie's delicate lace panties off and drew the head of his erection up and down her slick folds, tantalising her, torturing himself, until she was slick and hot. Too impatient to wait, she rose up and took him in her hand, then slowly slid down, taking all of him inside her body. It was so exquisite Arkim had to grit his jaw tightly.

They moved with a kind of slow but languorous intent…rocking, sliding…and when the need became too great Arkim held Sylvie's hips in place and lost himself inside her, burying his head in her breast, feeling her hands on his head, as his soul flew apart and finally he found the oblivion he was looking for.

A couple of hours later Sylvie was lying on her side, naked, her hands under her face, watching Arkim's chest rise and fall. He'd taken her to bed and made love to her again, and the after-shocks of pleasure still pulsed through her body at intermittent intervals. The intensity of the way he'd taken her on the couch still took her breath away. It was as if he'd been consumed with a kind of fury.

His face was in profile to her, showing the proud line of his nose. From here she couldn't see his injured eye. Sylvie couldn't help but feel that in spite of the passion with which Arkim had taken her just now something had altered since that confrontation at the hotel.

A cold weight settled in her belly as an ugly reminder reared its head. She'd been meaning to discuss something with Arkim for the past couple of days and had been avoiding it like a coward. Because she was afraid that it would prove to be some kind of a test. A test of where she really fitted into his life.

As his chest rose and fell evenly she envied him his peace, when *her* body and brain felt as if they were tying themselves into a million knots. Knowing she wouldn't rest, Sylvie slipped out of bed and got dressed, going into the living room.

She sat cross-legged on the couch and Omar jumped up into her lap. As she petted him absently and looked into the muted darkness she knew that she had no choice but to talk to Arkim. And after what had happened this evening she knew that he would have no hesitation in letting her go. For good, this time.

Dawn was breaking outside when Arkim woke. His head was throbbing and he wondered why—until he lifted a hand and winced when it came into contact with his black eye.

Sylvie. Anger jerked him fully awake in an instant. The memory of those men…eating her up with their eyes. And one of them had touched her. He'd seen it. His hands curled into fists just from thinking about it, remembering, his blood pressure increasing.

No woman had ever roused Arkim to the point

of wanting to do violence on her behalf. But he'd been ready to take on all those men. His anger had been volcanic. It was something he hadn't felt in a long time...since the day that woman had controlled him for her own amusement and his father had thrown him out like unwanted baggage.

Sylvie. Arkim looked around. He was alone in the room...no sounds were coming from the bathroom. He wanted her even now, even after making love to her like some kind of feral youth on the couch earlier. Damn her. Would he *ever* not want her?

Not wanting to investigate the way his gut clenched at that prospect, Arkim got out of bed and pulled on a pair of sweats, feeling as if he'd done about ten rounds in a boxing ring. He frowned as he padded through the apartment, hearing nothing but silence. Not even Omar.

He checked all the rooms and came to the living room last—and finally he saw her. She was standing with her back to the door, looking out of the window. He noticed that she was dressed in jeans and a shirt. There was something tense about the lines of her body that made him stay where he was.

'You're dressed.'

The lines of Sylvie's body got tenser. She turned around slowly. Her hair was pulled into a low bun at the back of her head. She confounded him—she could go from looking like the sexiest movie star goddess to something like this, much more simple and plain, and yet his body reacted the same way every time.

He leaned against the door and crossed his arms, grateful for the fact that his sweats were loose. His susceptibility to this woman was something that still made him feel uncomfortable. Exposed.

Sylvie's arms were crossed too. 'There was something I wanted to tell you earlier, but I never got a chance.'

Feeling a flutter of panic, and not liking it, Arkim said, 'Is it so important it can't wait till later?' He stood up straight and held out a hand. 'Come back to bed...it's too early for talk.'

Sylvie smiled, but it was touched with something Arkim hadn't seen in some time. Cynicism. 'No, it can't wait...'

Arkim went over to the drinks cabinet and helped himself to a shot of brandy. He saluted Sylvie. 'Medicinal purposes.'

She paled at that, and Arkim paused with the glass halfway to his mouth. 'What is it?'

She looked at him, that blue-green gaze unnervingly direct. 'Pierre has offered me a bigger role in the show.'

The tight ball in Arkim's gut seemed to ease. *That was it?* 'That sounds good.' So why did she look so serious?

'It is good... But if I accept it I'll have to take off my clothes for the first time...like the other girls. Pierre has never pressured me about this before... I told you, he's been like a father to me. But he says now that if I want to stay I have to start delivering a fuller performance.'

For a second Arkim just heard a roaring in his ears. Images rushed through his head: Sylvie's pale breasts bared for thousands of people to see... Her perfect body... No wonder her boss wanted to exploit her.

And those men last night...they would look at her—every night if they wished. And taunt Arkim with the knowledge that they'd seen as much of his lover as he had.

He realised his hand had tightened so much around the glass that he risked breaking it. He forced himself to relax, to focus.

Sylvie continued. 'The truth is that I don't know

if I should do it or not. I've been thinking…about doing something else.'

Relief vied with something much darker inside Arkim. Sylvie was looking at him far too carefully. As if his response mattered. As if she wanted him to tell her what to do.

The sheer volatility of his emotions was like acid in his stomach, inhibiting his response. If he told Sylvie he cared what she did she would have control over him…she would know his vulnerability. It would make a statement about what was happening here, would demonstrate a possessiveness of her that had already earned him a black eye. In public. In front of his peers.

He went cold—because he hadn't even contemplated that side of it yet.

He'd just weathered one public scandal…was he now in danger of being dragged into another one?

It was too much. Too reminiscent of that day when he'd lost his innocence and his self-respect. When he'd been found, literally, with his pants down and that woman's mouth around his— He blanked the poisonous memory. He wasn't going back there for anyone.

Carefully, he took a sip of his drink. He didn't even feel the burn. His voice when he spoke was cool. Calm. Belying the tumult underneath. 'I don't really know what you want me to say. It's your life, Sylvie. You should do whatever you think is best for you.'

She looked at him for a long moment, but it was a kind of dead-eyed stare. She was so pale that Arkim almost made a move towards her, but then she seemed to break out of her trance-like state and uncrossed her arms, her gaze narrowed.

'Yes, it *is* my life, and I *do* know what's best for me. Which is why I'm going to leave now.'

Arkim frowned. 'Leave...?'

Sylvie glanced down to where Omar was sitting at her feet, looking up at her adoringly, his tongue hanging out. But she didn't bend down to pick him up. Arkim saw her hands form fists, as if to stop herself.

She looked back at him, her jaw tight. 'Yes, leave. The new show opens in a week and there's a huge PR campaign starting tomorrow. In light of what happened last night I think it's best if we call it quits now.' Her chin lifted. 'I would prefer not to be responsible for any further public incidents, and when the new show takes off... Well, it's only more likely to happen.'

Something hard and dark and cold settled into

Arkim's belly. 'So you're going to do it, then? Take Pierre up on his offer?'

Her face was like a pale smooth mask. She shrugged lightly. 'It's all I've ever known. They're my family...I'd be a fool not to want to progress in one of the most famous shows in the world.'

'By taking off your clothes?' Arkim almost spat the words.

Sylvie's gaze sparked. 'What's it to you? I have to worry about my career, Arkim. If I don't take this opportunity now there's a million girls coming up behind me who'll do the job.'

Arkim had to grit his jaw. He wanted to say, *What about the way you were dancing that day when I found you again?*

She had been so passionate and beautiful. But that wasn't really her, was it? If she was prepared to do this? Take the last step over the line...? Something within Arkim snapped and the words spilled out before he could stop them. 'What if I asked you to stay?'

A flare of colour came into Sylvie's cheeks. 'How long for? Another week? A month? Two months? We both know what this is...impermanent. Unless...'

Unless it's more.

The implication of her unfinished sentence made Arkim say harshly, 'Unless it's nothing.'

'It's nothing, then,' said Sylvie faintly.

She walked over and picked up her bag and a jacket, shrugging into it in jerky movements. She was avoiding Arkim's eye as she walked to the other side of the room, where he saw that a larger bag was waiting. So she'd packed already. Because she'd known how he would react? The knowledge sent a sharp pain through his chest.

She turned around to face him, looking very petite and young. Delicate. He thought of her just a couple of hours ago, astride him, rocking her body against his. She'd been like a fearsome warrior, claiming her pleasure with a ferocity matched only by Arkim's desire to give it to her.

The image was so vivid that it took him a second to realise she'd gone.

No.

He put down the glass, uncaring that it fell to the floor, spilling dark golden liquid. When he got to the hall, he saw her holding Omar close, burying her face in his body before putting him down carefully. Something was constricting Arkim, like a band around his chest.

She didn't face him. She put her hand on the

knob of the door and said tautly, 'I can't take him with me—it's not practical... But you will take care of him, won't you?'

Arkim was cold. All over. He hated his father. He'd never known his mother. He'd never known love. What he felt for Sylvie was just too...*overwhelming*.

'Of course.'

He wasn't even aware that he'd spoken. Cold was good. This was what he wanted. He didn't want volatility. Messy passion. *Emotions*.

'Thank you. Goodbye, Arkim.' She opened the door, and just before she stepped through she said huskily, 'Take care of yourself.'

After she'd gone Arkim was dimly aware of something warm on his toes, and he looked down stupidly to see Omar, tail wagging, making a small pitiful sound. He bent down and scooped him up against his chest, then went into the living room and sat on the couch, where the puppy settled trustingly into his lap.

He could smell Sylvie's delicate scent on the air. And something else. *Sex*. He realised that this was where he'd had her...only hours before. Every time he'd lost himself inside her it had felt as if another part of his soul was being altered.

He clenched his jaw so hard it hurt. Pain was good. The pain reminded him that he craved order and respectability above all. He didn't *need* his soul to be altered.

Sylvie Devereux had been a brief and torrid interlude in his life and now he was moving on. For good.

CHAPTER ELEVEN

A week later—L'Amour revue, final dress rehearsal...

'*SYLVIE!* HURRY UP! You're next.'

Sylvie took a deep breath, grabbed her prop sword, and made her way to the spotlit stage. The mood was controlled chaos. The new show was opening in a few hours and they still had lots to prepare. She was in a more elaborate version of the belly dance outfit that she'd worn for Arkim in Al-Hibiz, and the reminder was jarring.

When she got on stage the music started almost at once, so she had to jump straight into the routine. She wasn't overly worried about how precise her movements were because this rehearsal was really for the technical team, to make sure that all the timings for cues and lights and so on were lined up properly.

She had taken off her veil and head-covering and pushed her sword away, ready to move into the second part of the dance, when a loud *'Stop!'* sounded in the dark theatre.

Sylvie's heart stuttered, but she told herself she was imagining that she knew the voice. She was on her feet now and she kept going. It was probably just one of the stage hands.

Suddenly the music stopped.

She whirled around to hear some kind of a scuffle going on in the darkness backstage, and then a man walked out onto the stage from behind the curtains. Even though he was in the shadow of the lights she knew it was Arkim, taller and broader than everyone else.

He was holding something that looked like a vital piece of audio equipment. Sure enough, he was quickly followed by an irate sound engineer, spluttering and gesticulating furiously, grabbing back his piece of equipment and disappearing again.

Sylvie wasn't sure she wasn't dreaming. 'Arkim...?'

He stepped forward into the spotlight. He wasn't a mirage. And then she became aware of the fact that they had an audience of crew and other dancers.

'What the hell are you doing? We're in the middle of rehearsals—you can't be here,' she hissed at him. But her mind leapt to the million and one possibilities of why he might be there anyway.

She noticed that the swelling on his eye had gone down, to be replaced by a dark bruise. He looked as if he'd just come from a brawl in an alley.

Her fault.

And, adding to her sense of everything being unreal, he was wearing faded worn denims and a close-fitting T-shirt, more casual than she'd ever seen him. It was almost as shocking as the time when she'd seen him naked in the pool at the oasis. His hair was messy and his overall demeanour was edgy and dangerous. He looked a million miles removed from the man she'd first seen in her father's house in his three-piece suit, so controlled. So disdainful.

'Arkim—'

But he cut her off, saying baldly, 'I don't want you to strip. I don't want anyone else to see you.'

Shock reverberated through her. And something scarily like euphoria. But just as quickly she feared that she was reading this all wrong.

She put her hands on her hips, anger flaring. 'It's okay for *you* to see me, but you're so controlling and possessive that you can't bear the thought that your *ex*-property might become a little more public?'

He stepped closer, the inevitable electricity sparking between them. 'No,' he growled. 'I don't want anyone to see you because you're *mine*.'

Sylvie glared up at him. 'Do I need to remind you that you've let me go—*twice*?' The knowledge of her own weakness around him and the realisation that he'd never choose her to be a permanent part of his life made her say frigidly, 'What is it, Arkim? You're so concerned with your precious reputation that you're afraid my debauched life-style will come back to haunt you?'

A muscle in his jaw pulsed. 'No, dammit. I don't want anyone else to see what's *mine*.'

Emotion made Sylvie's chest ache. This man had started out rejecting her before he'd even known her, and even after getting to know her— intimately—he'd still ultimately rejected her. He was just here beating his chest because he couldn't bear the thought of sharing her.

'But I'm not *yours*. You let me go.'

They were so close now they were almost touching. Sylvie was unaware of anything but the man in front of her and those deep, dark eyes. Eyes that could look so cold and dead, but which she knew could turn her heart upside down and inside out.

'I don't want you to go. I want you to stay.'

Hating the little tremor of emotion that made her heart jump with irrational hope, Sylvie threw out a hand. 'We've *had* this conversation. For how long? Another two weeks? A month? And then you'll move on with your perfect respectable life and you'll meet some perfect respectable woman and you'll marry her—like you wanted to marry Sophie because she was so perfect for you.'

'*You* are perfect for me.'

Sylvie's mouth was still open. She shut it abruptly, aghast at everything that had tumbled out. And had he just said...?

'What did you say?'

'I said that you are perfect for me. I don't want anyone else.'

His words impacted like a sledgehammer, knocking her to pieces. And even though she'd registered them she shook her head, took a step back. It wasn't hard to envisage being rejected again, when Arkim woke up one morning and realised she wasn't perfect for him, wasn't really suitable for the life he wanted, and this time his rejection would be comprehensive and fatal.

She wouldn't recover. And the worst of it was she *knew* why it was so important to him...she wanted him to be happy.

'This is just lust talking,' she said.

Before Sylvie could react Arkim had closed the distance between them and cupped her face in his hands. He blotted out the world when he lowered his mouth to hers. Sylvie might have expected devastation, bruising passion...but his kiss was like a kind of benediction. A kiss that was gentle and restrained, but with the unmistakable promise of *more*.

And, damn him, she couldn't help but respond. A sob of reaction was working its way up her throat, making her grab his T-shirt in order to stay standing. She just wasn't able to defend herself. The last week had been torture.

Eventually Arkim pulled back, his eyes glittering down into hers. Sylvie felt exposed...vulnerable.

'I know what I want and I want you.'

I want. Not *I love.* And Sylvie needed love. After feeling so bruised all her life from her father's rejection, she couldn't go through that with someone else. Better to be the rejecter. Arkim didn't want her. Not really. No matter what he said or how he kissed her.

She pulled free. 'It wasn't enough of a wake-up call that you got punched in the face? Are you so blinded that you've forgotten what I do? What I am? Wherever we go there's always going to be a risk that someone will recognise me...' She crossed her fingers behind her back at the white lie she was about to tell. 'And especially when I become famous for taking my clothes off completely. I won't be one of the less risqué acts any more, Arkim. Everyone will know what I look like naked.'

Sylvie could see him pale slightly under the olive tones of his skin. His face was starker, leaner than she'd ever seen it. As if he'd lost weight in the space of a week.

'If that's what you really want to do I won't pretend that I'll like it, but I'll support you.'

Sylvie reeled. Her jaw dropped. Eventually she got out, 'You're saying you'd *accept* me, no matter what?' She couldn't believe it for a second. Because if she did... Her heart contracted painfully.

She shook her head. 'This is not you talking... This is lust...desire. And once it's gone, Arkim—' Her voice broke traitorously. 'I won't let you send me away again when you realise that I'm not perfect after all…because I'm a constant reminder of some weakness you feel, of your life with your father.'

She'd moved to turn away, her vision blurring, when Arkim's hand shot out and caught her shoulder. She saw Pierre standing and watching, his gnarled old face incredulous. They had an avid audience. Everyone had gathered to watch the show.

Sylvie let Arkim turn her back towards him, saying in a choked voice, 'Arkim, you have to—'

'Stop talking, Sylvie.'

Her mouth closed. He had to know they were being observed. Why wasn't he leaving? Why wasn't he preserving what was left intact of his reputation?

Maybe because he means what he says? said a small seductive voice.

But before she could do or say anything more Arkim was reaching for the bottom of his T-shirt, pulling it up over his head and off, revealing his very taut and perfect musculature.

There was a collective intake of appreciative breath and a low whistle, which sounded as if it was quickly stifled by an elbow in the ribs.

Sylvie barely noticed, she was so shocked. 'What are you *doing*?'

His hands were on his jeans now. He looked grim. 'I'm trying to prove to you that I'll do whatever it takes to make you trust in me.'

He was starting to undo his top button, and Sylvie realised that he fully intended to strip completely. She put out a shaking hand. 'Stop.' And then she shook her head. 'Why…?'

Arkim dropped his hands, and now he looked bleak. 'Because I need to show you that I'm willing to bare myself totally for you. And that if you wanted me to stand in front of Notre Dame and do it, I would. I need you to know that I won't ever judge you again. I'm proud of you, and of everything you've achieved with such innate dignity and pride. You shame me. Everything I've been aiming for my whole life is empty. Meaningless. Without you.'

Sylvie was struck dumb.

He seared her alive with the intensity in his dark gaze. 'Don't you get it yet? I love you… But it took me a really long time to understand it because I've never loved anyone, so I didn't know what it felt like…and I'm sorry.'

To her absolute shock Arkim proceeded to get

down on one knee in front of her. He took something out of his pocket. A small velvet box. He opened it up and took something out, held it up between his fingers. She could see that his hand was trembling.

He took her hand in his and said, 'Sylvie Devereux, I know I've given you every reason in the world to hate me...but will you please consent to be my wife? Because I love you, and without you I'm just an arrogant, uptight prat.' He squeezed her hand. 'Whatever it is you want to do in this life I will support you, and I will take a thousand blows for you if that's what comes my way. Because you're mine to protect and cherish and love, and I pledge to do this for as long as I have breath in my body.'

Sylvie felt dizzy, anchored to the earth only by Arkim's hand wrapped around hers. She wasn't even looking at the ring, glinting with a green flash of colour in her peripheral vision. She wanted to believe...*so* badly. And then she realised that she was just as guilty as he of wanting to protect herself. She had to trust or she'd never move on from her old hurts.

She spoke with a rush. 'I'm not really taking Pierre's offer...I just said that to try and make you see how inappropriate I was for you. I'm only performing tonight as a favour, because we're stuck for an act. My modern dance teacher is putting together a company, here in Paris, and he wants me to be a part of it—as one of their lead dancers. I won't be taking my clothes off, but I still won't be perfect.'

He smiled a crooked smile. 'You *are* perfect. If you want to ride naked on a horse through the streets of Paris then I'll take off all my clothes too and join you.'

Another voluble sigh came from someone nearby. Sylvie ignored it.

Arkim's hand gripped hers. 'I just want you to be happy...'

And finally it sank in, and spread through her whole body like a warm glow, lighting up the dark corners that had been filled with pain and uncertainty for a long time.

Sylvie realised that Arkim was looking a little strained... He was still waiting for her answer. Unsure.

'Yes,' she said softly, her heart swelling. 'Yes, I'll marry you.' She got down on her knees and faced him, touching his face, tracing his mouth. She looked at him and said shakily, 'I love you so, much…I think I've loved you for ever. And I knew it the moment I saw you, even though I couldn't understand how…'

For a second Arkim looked stunned, as if he truly hadn't known what she would say. Then she felt him push the ring on her finger, and glanced down to see a huge emerald flanked by smaller blue sapphires and diamonds. Like her eyes.

She reached for him just as he reached for her, their mouths fusing, bodies pressed close enough to hurt.

And then a very loud and obvious cough from nearby made Sylvie jerk in Arkim's arms. The theatre and their surroundings filtered back into her consciousness as if she were coming out of a particularly delicious dream.

She looked around to see a sea of faces and a lot of suspiciously shiny eyes. Pierre, however, looked familiarly stern. But she could see the glint of affection in his expression.

He eyeballed Arkim. 'If you've quite finished with my dancer, Mr Al-Sahid, I have a theatre to run and a show to put on in less than an hour…'

Arkim had a tight grip on Sylvie's hips and he was still unashamedly half naked. Something Sylvie was becoming more and more burningly aware of. The ring he'd put on her finger felt heavy and solid. A happy weight.

Arkim, totally unfazed by Pierre, looked at Sylvie. 'There's nothing I want more than to take you home right now...but do you want to do the show?'

The Arkim she'd first met might have carried her out of here over his shoulder. Or paid Pierre to release her.

Sylvie looked between the men and then back to Arkim. Her voice was husky when she said, 'Yes, I'd like to do it. It's to be my last performance, and it's thanks to Pierre I got a place with the modern dance company.' Sylvie grinned. 'He only offered me the bigger role because he knew I'd say no and that it was the push I needed to move on...'

Arkim looked at the older man, his eyes suspiciously bright. He stood up and, bringing Sylvie with him, reached out to shake the man's hand. 'Thank you for taking care of her—and for seeing her potential.'

Now Pierre looked suspiciously emotional. Sylvie fought back her own tears and pulled away from Arkim. She had to finish getting ready. He let her go with a look that told her he'd be in the front row, waiting for her. For ever.

Just before Sylvie went out of earshot, though, she thought she heard Pierre say hopefully, 'Mr Al-Sahid, are you *sure* you don't have any dance experience...?'

EPILOGUE

THE PRIEST'S EYES widened as he took in the spectacle approaching down the aisle. There was the slim figure of the bride, dressed from head to toe in white satin and lace, her face obscured by a gauzy veil. Her arm was tucked into the arm of the young woman who was giving her away. She was blonde and very pretty, dressed in dusky pink, and—the priest frowned—very familiar. Because, he realised, he'd watched *her* come down the aisle dressed as a bride only a few short months before. To stand with the same groom.

The groom now turned to look and the priest could sense his nervous tension. He hadn't been half as jumpy the last time.

The woman in pink handed the bride over to the groom with a smile and a look that said, *Take care of her or I'll kill you*. But the priest could tell that the groom needed no such warning. He looked as if he'd kill anyone who dared to come between him and this woman, who was now stepping up to the altar, her hand firmly in his.

But then, before the priest could open his mouth to start the proceedings, the groom lifted the veil from his bride's radiant face and pushed it over her head, before pulling her close to lower his head and press a kiss to her mouth.

Eventually, after realising that this was the same woman who had so sensationally interrupted the last wedding, the priest coughed loudly. They separated, the bride's face flushed, her eyes shining.

The priest was feeling rather hot under the collar by now himself, and said testily, 'If you're quite ready, shall we proceed?'

They both looked at him and the groom smiled. 'We're ready.'

And thankfully, when the moment came for anyone to object, there was nothing but happy silence...

* * * * *

0616 Rom LP

MILLS & BOON®
Large Print – August 2016

The Sicilian's Stolen Son
Lynne Graham

Seduced into Her Boss's Service
Cathy Williams

The Billionaire's Defiant Acquisition
Sharon Kendrick

One Night to Wedding Vows
Kim Lawrence

Engaged to Her Ravensdale Enemy
Melanie Milburne

A Diamond Deal with the Greek
Maya Blake

Inherited by Ferranti
Kate Hewitt

The Billionaire's Baby Swap
Rebecca Winters

The Wedding Planner's Big Day
Cara Colter

Holiday with the Best Man
Kate Hardy

Tempted by Her Tycoon Boss
Jennie Adams